Legac[y] of the

Dragonwand

Book I

Legacy of

Dragonwand

Book I

By Daniel Peyton

Cosby Media Productions

Entertaining the Mind, and Inspiring the Soul

Cosby Media Productions™

Entertaining the Mind, and Inspiring the Soul

The opinions expressed by the author are not necessarily those of Cosby Media Productions.

Published by Cosby Media Productions.

www.cosbymediaproductions.com

Cover art: Cosby Media Productions

Edited: Tamar Hela

ISBN-13: 978-0692642047

ISBN-10: 0692642048

TABLE OF CONTENTS

A teenage would-be wizard just wants to go to wizard school, but he finds himself on an epic quest instead...all the standard elements of a YA fantasy protagonist's transformation into a hero - **KIRKUS REVIEWS**

PROLOGUE

THE earth-shaking bellow of a dragon caused Markus to jump to the ground in fear. Trembling all over, he cautiously lifted his head just as a golden dragon unleashed a volley of fire at an obsidian black dragon. The obsidian dragon shot back with greenish hellfire. It was so great, it exploded as far as Markus could see. He scrunched up his body in an attempt to avoid being burned alive.

Markus looked up again to find himself in the eye of a firestorm; greenish black fire was mixing with yellow and orange fire. The ground vibrated hard under his feet, and the earsplitting screams of the dragons fighting was almost more than he could handle.

At once, a huge black claw swooped down into the fires and scooped Markus up. The dark dragon held him so tight that he could barely breathe. The beast yelled out, "YOU HAVE LOST!"

"HE WILL COME!" the golden dragon replied, and then swooped over the fires and came up fast on the obsidian dragon. The golden dragon grabbed its foe by the tail, then opened its maw to release a flurry of flames.

Markus struggled for air and clenched his eyes closed as the light orange fire washed over him. Oddly, the world went cold and the feel of the claws around his ribs was gone.

Markus shot up in his bed. He gasped a few times before he realized his body had not been clutched by a dragon. The sound of the battle seemed to still be in his ears, though the ringing faded quickly. Taking a few breaths to make sure his lungs still worked, his fear faded more quickly than the sounds in his head. It had been a terrible, traumatizing nightmare, just like the many others he'd had since his earliest childhood memories.

"What time is it?" he mumbled to himself.

Out of the nearest window, he could see that the rainstorm from last night had passed and the first hints of sunlight were illuminating the distant horizon. Morning wasn't far off, and his father would be getting up soon to tend to the farm duties. If Markus was going to leave home, now was the time.

After placing a letter on the kitchen table and packing a bag, Markus left his home in search of a better future.

CHAPTER 1: SEARCHING FOR A WIZARD

HANDSOME, fifteen-year-old Markus was born into a family of farmers. It was a simple life that he wasn't overly fond of. He had always dreamed of becoming something greater than a farmer. From his earliest childhood memory until today, he had been plagued with dreams that fascinated and confused him. There were dreams of magic, dragons, spells, and other fantastic things. At times, they were nightmares, and at other times, they were adventures. But Markus knew one thing for sure: they weren't just dreams.

As he grew, he began to realize he had magical powers and some of the spells he dreamed of, he could perform—at least, on a small scale. His grandmother had magical powers and decided to deny them, as did his father. But Markus wanted to learn more. The only way he could learn what his dreams meant and how he could become a wizard was to join the Wizardry College. There was just the matter of getting a letter of recommendation.

So, Markus set off to find a way to get into the Wizardry College at Thendor. He needed to find the shack where the Wizard Tolen was rumored to live. There, he would make his request for the letter of recommendation. He packed a bag of dried fruits, nuts, and hard bread, then left for a week-long journey around the lowlands. He told his parents that if he did not return, it meant he was on his way to Thendor.

Markus walked along the dirt roads, passing farms and mills. The river was on his right, while green grasses and fragrant fields were on his left. Some of the aromas were lovely, and others were popular only among flies. But what would the farming community be without pigs, goats, and cows?

"Hey, Markusss!"A green-skinned farmer waved his hand at the boy.

Markus walked over to him and put on a feigned smile. This man was not the kindest person around. "Hello, Tolk."

Tolk, a Lizardkind, stretched his serpentine lips in the semblance of a smile. "Sssso, still sssearching for the old wizard'ssss cottage?"

Markus nodded. "Yes. I turn sixteen in a few weeks, and I have to get apprenticed to a school soon, or I'll be too old."

Tolk slithered out his tongue. "You really think you can convinsssss the old wizard to sssssponsor you?"

"Yes," Markus stated with squared shoulders and a firm expression.

"You are an ambitiousss fool, but sstill a fool. What if you anger him?" Tolk swished his long, scaly tail back and forth behind him.

"I'll convince him he has nothing to lose by sponsoring me. It's just a letter."

Tolk laughed with a hissing sound. "Ssstupid pink sssskin. That old wizard jusssst might turn you into a radissssh."

Markus glared at the man hissing and laughing on the other side of the short wooden fence. "I already know a few spells!"

Tolk just laughed, so Markus decided to prove himself. He held out his hand toward the ground and yelled out, "ELDR!"A puff of fire emitted from his palm and struck the dirt. It was hardly enough to ignite kindling, but it was enough to get the jerk to stop laughing.

Tolk jumped up and hissed harshly at Markus, "Damned pink ssssssskin!"

"Have fun scooping manure." With that, Markus left.

The sky warmed up as the day quickly headed toward noon. Markus felt like his feet were going to fall off. He had been walking for over a day and had found nothing but more farms. Never had he traveled so far in his life. The farther he got away from home, the more nervous he was.

"Wow, would you look at that." Markus stopped on the road and looked up at the mountain range forming the southern and eastern border of the valley. The densely forested mountains still had the early morning fog lifting up as the sun rose higher. In the middle of one section, the mountain had been removed and a stone gate built into the wall of rock. The gate was huge—larger than any building Markus had ever seen.

The gate itself was a marvel that defied much of what history recorded. It had a circular opening with two massive doors, which allowed passage. The wall around the doors was made up of giant cubes of stone cut and fitted together. Carved into the wall of bricks was a long snake, which wound around the gate and held the opening in its giant mouth. This gave the gate its name: Serpent's Gate. The Shlan, who once ruled over the lowlands, had built the gates to keep an eye on the flow of traffic through their lands.

"Quite impressive, isn't it?" an old voice said, startling Markus.

An elderly man with a long walking stick and a crooked smile stood beside him. Out one side of his mouth hung a long, thin pipe with just the slightest amount of smoke rising from it.

Markus regained his composure enough to ask, "Where did you come from?"

"Oh, I was takin' a walk. I enjoy lookin' at this old pass. The name's Wickers, but most people just call me Old Man. Ha!" He was a strange fellow.

"I see. Uh, my name's Markus. I was just traveling through."

"Most folks are just travelin' through these parts. The Port of

Pearls is on the other side of that pass. Don't suppose you're headin' that way?"

"Not sure."

Wickers took a puff on his pipe and gave Markus a funny look. "Not sure? Don'cha know where you're goin'?"

"Not really. I was looking for the wizard . . ."

"Was? Did ya find one?" Wickers interrupted.

Markus cleared his throat and tried again. "I *am* looking for the wizard I heard about in the valley, when I came upon this gate. I've read about this place before, but have never seen it."

Wickers took his pipe out and pointed the end at the gate. "That there gate is a big ol' mystery. None of your books really knows all about it."

"I know it was built by the Shlan before the Great War. I also know it hasn't been closed in almost a thousand years."

"Oh, so you do know somethin' 'bout it. But there's more." Wickers took a puff on his pipe. "See how it's built? That ain't no normal walkin' pass in the mountains. It was built for ships."

"Ships?" Markus scoffed. "There isn't enough water in this river to let ships pass through. I doubt it had much in the past either."

"Nope, this old river never had enough water to float a raft down.

7

Nope, nope. I ain't talkin' about sailing ships; I'm talkin' about flying ships."

"Flying ships? Come on." Now Markus was sure this old man was just making stuff up.

"No, really. Long time back, there was a big ol' empire in these here lands stretched far and wide to parts we ain't been yet. How you suppose they got around such a big empire? Flyin' ships. Air ships like sailing ships, could soar in the sky. The Shlan were tradin' partners with that empire and built this here gate to let in the cargo ships. Long before the War, the Lost Empire busted up. Then, the War came, the Shlan joined Gallenor, and they forgot this gate. Nobody seen a flyin' ship since."

Markus still didn't believe him. "What about that path? It leads right up to the entrance and through the gate . . . I think?"

"Put there by the Gallenorians to make travel easier. Climbin' through that gate must've been mighty hard without a flyin' ship, so they put dirt down until they had enough to walk on, all the way through. Got 'em to the Port of Pearls quicker."

"And just how do you know all of this?" Markus found the old man amusing.

Wickers stuck his pipe in his mouth and matter of factly stated, "I'm old. I know stuff."

"A thousand years old?" Markus teased him.

Wickers puffed on his pipe. "Maybe." Then he let out a big laugh.

Markus laughed as well. "Fine. I think I'll fly right through that pass and see if I can find a wizard in the port city."

Suddenly, Wickers stopped being so jovial. "A wizard?! There ain't any wizards in Pearls. Ain't any wizards anywhere."

"What?" Markus wasn't sure if Wickers was pulling his leg or was telling the truth. "But I have to find one."

"Well, I'm just an old man, but I ain't seen any wizards around the port in a long time. I haven't been there in a while, though."

Markus looked back at the gate and thought about Wicker's claims. "Then maybe I can find one."

Wickers became more serious as he puffed on his long pipe. "You would go to the port to find a wizard? Son, that city is dangerous. You wouldn't survive a day in a place like that."

"I'm stronger than you think. Besides, what trouble can I get into looking for a wizard?"

"In a place like Port of Pearls," Wickers mused. "Plenty. No, no, no good. Take my advice: head into the trees. If a wizard's gonna be any place around here, he's gonna be in the trees."

"The trees? Why?"

9

"Just makes sense. Travelers say they see a cottage in the forest belonging to an old wizard. Never seen it personally, but I don't get off the road too much these days."

Markus looked back down the road and saw that the hills to the west were thick with forests. He would be heading toward home again, but it would still be on his mission. "All right, I'll try the forest."

"Well then, young man, get on yer way. Don't keep your wizard waiting. Oh, and watch out for imps; they love the trees at night. Good luck!" He laughed heartily and continued walking toward the Serpent Gate.

Markus found himself amused and bewildered by this traveler. He was probably a crazy old coot, but what he said had been entertaining, even if it was all a tall tale. Markus turned around to say goodbye but found Wickers was already gone. "Wow, fast for an old fellow. Oh, well. I guess I'll see what's in these trees."

After a two-day walk through the valley and up into the hills, Markus was becoming worried he might never find the wizard's cottage. The rumors of it being found by travelers might have just been tall tales. No, he had to believe it was out here. He had to have faith.

Sitting on a stump, Markus folded his arms and considered what he was doing. He would not go home defeated. His parents had argued with him for so long about him staying when he wanted to leave, that he wasn't going to give them the pleasure of saying, "I told you so." Just because his father and grandmother denied their true nature did not mean *he* had to. He knew he had it in him, but he also knew his parents and grandparents had given up. They had settled for being lowly farmers. If Markus walked home now, he would walk home to a life of mundane farming and barely scraping to get by. Going out to the Port of Pearls wasn't the brightest idea either. He acted brave, but he knew he would not survive in a city like that alone.

Just then, he heard a rumbling. It was him. He let out a sorrowful sigh and checked his bag. He wasn't even close to being out of food, but he was terribly tired of eating dried fruits and nuts.

While munching, he looked out over the valley. Even though he might not have had the desire to make farming his life, he did love the view. This valley, known locally as only the lowlands, was situated as a bowl amongst mountains and hills. A river cut through the valley, gently bending and curving a path from a waterfall at the northern side, to another waterfall at the southern side. The valley itself was flat and bright green with soil perfect for farming. Thus, the land had been the location of farms for eons, long before the founding of Gallenor, in fact.

11

From this higher altitude, Markus saw what few really noticed while going about their daily chores. The farms made the land look like a big quilt, with different shades of greens and browns, where the different patches of land had been prepared and worked for whatever they were growing. Outside of the patchwork were large pastures that contained the livestock. The blue skies overhead, the birds chirping in the trees, and the sounds of hearty work down below, made this a picturesque valley.

"Good grief!" Markus shivered and wrapped his arms around himself.

The wind was so bitter, he was sure frost fairies were near him, though they were just myths these days. The wind made an odd sound—a sound that was hard to understand precisely—but Markus was sure he heard words. Suddenly, the cold breezes stopped. It was far too abrupt to be a natural occurrence. He looked around to see what could have saved him from the shrill cold. To his shock and amazement, a little house sat amongst the trees, as though it had been here all along. It was made of stone and wood, with a crooked chimney. Green moss and vines had overtaken most of the surface and crystals were strung up all around it as decorations.

"This is it!" Markus jumped up from where he sat to eat, discovering he had come upon the wizard's cottage. After a moment of excitement, he realized he was talking to no one and composed himself. If he were to address an honored wizard, he would have to do so with humble dignity.

As Markus approached the house, he became understandably nervous. If this wizard had been hiding, he was doing so for a good reason. What if approaching meant death?! No, he had to be positive. No one had reported such terrible things. And, after a quick look around, Markus noted no bones were lying about the ground.

With a shaking hand, he slowly knocked on the door. The knock was so soft, he hardly heard it himself. He was just about to knock again when the door slowly creaked open. Either he was welcome, or the door wasn't entirely closed and he had just dislodged it.

"Hello?" came a squeaky little voice out of his mouth. No response. He cautiously took a step into the cabin, cleared his throat and said again, "Hello? Is anyone here?"

"Morris, is that you?" a weak, raspy voice called out.

"No, it is I, Markus."

"Markus? I know no Markus. Is this a trick? I warn you, I can still do great things!"

Markus gulped. "It's no trick, sir. I'm truly Markus of the Valley. I've come to find the wizard Tolen, to make a request of him."

"You speak with honesty, young Markus. Come in."

Markus carefully stepped in and looked around. The voice was weak, yet vibrated throughout the house, so he wasn't sure where to find the wizard. The door closed behind him with a slam and then latched itself locked.

Looking around, Markus was astounded by the magic. The room was filled to the brim with crystals, plants, bright colored liquids, and odd bits of sculpted metal. It was like stepping into a dream, his dream of magic.

As he continued to look around, Markus saw a wind chime hanging in the middle of the room. He was captivated by the workmanship. With incredible artistic metal sculpting, the chime was made up of stars and other celestial objects, arranged to simulate an actual starry night.

"Wait there, Markus," the voice commanded.

Markus stopped directly beneath the chimes. "Sir? What do you want of me?"

"Markus of the Valley, what does your heart desire?"

Markus thought before answering, "My fondest desire is to be a wizard."

"Ah, I see. For good, or for evil?"

"I don't know. A good one, I guess. I've never thought about it much."

"There is more, I think. You need answers for something and

believe becoming a wizard will provide them." The old voice spoke with great wisdom.

Markus cleared his throat. "Since I was young, I've had dreams of magic. My father told me they were merely the effects of an overactive imagination. But a few years back, I discovered I could actually perform some of the spells from my dreams."

"You are afraid of your dreams. I can sense your hesitation over them."

Markus looked up at the chimes, curious about what they could be doing to him. "Not all of them, but some. I've seen dragons in my dreams, evil wizards, and even war. I don't know what the images mean. But I want to find out."

"When you do, what will you do with this information?"

"I don't know. It will depend upon what the information tells me. I do know that whatever I learn, my goal is to come back to the Valley and help the farmers by becoming the local wizard. We haven't had one in a long time and they need one. That's all."

"That's all?" The voice repeated his last words as if studying them, perhaps even entertained by them.

Just then, the chimes began to turn on the arms and strings holding them up. The metal parts met each other and made a perfect chord in the key of A. The old voice laughed. "I see, I see. You truly are an honest boy. But, you do not know your potential. You are to be a wizard, and a great one at that." There was a harsh coughing, and then he continued. "Come to me. I wish to bestow upon you what you need."

Markus was pleased. He was going to get his letter. He glanced around, hoping to see something to point him to this person. There, in a far corner, an old hand waved for him to approach. With a much more confident gait, Markus moved about the mystical cabin and found a very old man lying in a bed. The bed was in a cove with a window to one side.

The old man smiled at Markus. His ancient face was nearly bone and skin, nothing more. A heavy quilt covered most of him, except for his head, chest, and one bony arm.

"Young Markus. Do you know who I am?"

Markus shook his head. "I've heard you're Tolen, the wizard. But I don't know if this's true."

"It is." He coughed hard with a heavy rasp and then continued. "I am Tolen the Wise. Once the head wizard over the college. I founded that college just after the War."

"The War? There haven't been any wars in centuries."

"Yes, this is true. But what I said is also true."

Markus thought about the wizard's answer and then put the

numbers together. "Then you must be over a thousand years old!"

Tolen seemed to be embarrassed. "I should have passed on centuries ago, but my work was not done. Now, child, you must help me. Age has caught up with me and I cannot continue."

"What can I do for you, sir?"

Tolen pointed to the wall where a strange object hung. It was a long stick with a marble at the base end. Around its shaft, a twisted golden metal cord wound all the way to the top and was crafted into a strange, half-moon shape with the points at the ends coming together to hold onto another marble. It was a wand. "Take that, please."

Markus was scared. It was considered illegal for a non-wizard to hold a wand. "Sir, I'm no wizard. I'm asking to be allowed to learn. If I take this wand in my hands, I'll be breaking the law."

"Do not fear. I would not ask you to do this if it were not important. You will understand."

With a thumping heart and a fearful gulp, Markus did as he was asked. He reached up, grasped the wand by the shaft, and lifted it from the nails keeping it up on the wall. He held it for a moment and marveled at its lightweight, yet firm construction. It was beautiful, wonderful, and fearsome. He had dreamed of holding a wand, but only after training and the proper allowances.

With wide eyes, he asked, "What now?"

"Hand it to me," Tolen commanded.

Markus carefully gave the large wand to Tolen and waited. Tolen looked at the wand and then at the boy for a long time. He seemed to size him up as though he were not sure of him. Then a smile grew slowly across his face. He held out the wand, pointing it at Markus. "Markus of the Valley, I pass this wand to you."

The wand glowed, and then a ball of white energy flung toward Markus. He flinched, but felt nothing.

"Now, take it," Tolen said, holding out the wand.

Markus fearfully took the wand. "But, sir, I'm not yet a wizard. You must have me confused with someone else. I'm a boy from the farming village in the Valley. Not a great wizard. I don't even know many spells, and the ones I do know are sloppy and terribly weak," he rambled.

"You have within you a great deal of power." Tolen spoke firmly, saying, "This wand will provide you the strength you need."

Markus quickly replaced the wand on the wall and stepped back. "I'm sorry, but this is too much. I only wanted a letter." As he stepped back, the wand vanished from the nails it sat upon.

"This wand will lead you to the answers you seek," Tolen insisted.

This caught the boy's attention. "It will show me what my dreams mean?"

"Not by itself, but it will lead you to what will. Your dreams are very important. They are a key to your past and your future. If you do not unlock their meaning, you will live the rest of your life seeing their images in your sleep."

Markus looked around for the wand, becoming a bit panicked. "The wand!? I can't find it!"

"Worry not, young one. Calm down." Tolen tried to wave his hand at Markus, but he no longer had the strength to lift his arm. "Call it into your hand."

Markus frowned in confusion, but obliged. He held out his hand and said, "Wand." In a flash, the wand was in his hand. "What . . . how . . . did I just do that?"

"Yes. You do not even have to say it aloud." Tolen paused from the weakness that was turning deathly, and then continued to explain. "Simply think of it being in your hand, and it will appear. You cannot lose it, nor can anyone else hold it. It will slip through their fingers as a shadow."

Markus began to realize what had just transpired. He set the wand down on the bed and backed away, saying, "I . . . I . . . I . . . am not ready for this. I need training. This is too much. I can't . . ." As he

19

stepped farther away, the wand vanished again.

Tolen shook his head against the pillow. "No, young Markus. I chose you long ago. When I heard your heart calling for magic, I knew you would be the one I required."

"Months ago? How did you know?"

"I know much, child. I sent the call to your father's heart, and to your grandmother's, but they were afraid of magic and chose a simple life. You heard me and came."

"I heard nothing. I was simply seeking a wizard to give me a letter of sponsorship. Not this!" Markus was upset. This wasn't want he wanted. The wizard had given him an amazing responsibility by simply handing a wand over to him. Markus was young and afraid of being forced to grow up so fast.

"I know what you believe of yourself, but trust in your heart. You are capable of great things." He gave Markus a serious look. "Do you no longer wish to know the meanings behind your dreams?"

Markus thought for a moment and decided that his desires were still firm. "I do."

"What of learning about the magic within you?"

His answer came without a single hesitation. "Yes. I want to learn."

Tolen closed his eyes and struggled to take a breath. He opened his eyes again and looked upon Markus. "Child, you are the key to the future of Gallenor. Without you, this land is doomed, and all that we know of will be lost. Your dreams have a deeper meaning than you can possibly know. Use this wand to find the answers."

Markus' heart raced and his mind filled with every question imaginable. He made the choice to grow up and trust this man's words. With more confidence in his voice than he had displayed during the entire visit, he asked, "What do I do?"

"Complete a task of mine. During the journey, you will learn answers to your dreams and your life."

"What's this task?"

Tolen smiled, knowing he had his champion. "There is an ancient wand in the Dragon Citadel that needs to be retrieved and brought to the statue of the last dragon near Thendor."

"What's so special about this wand?"

Tolen let out a sorrowful sigh. "It is the last Dragonwand. Its power is unique and can be used to stop the dark tide that rises in Gallenor. I was on the cusp of finding it when the King suddenly became paranoid of wizards—me in particular. I was not allowed to finish my task, leaving the wand in the precarious position of being found by the wrong person."

"Do you think the King wants to find it to use it?" Markus found that hard to believe.

"I do not know what goes through that man's mind. I do know he is not to be trusted, nor are any of his loyal guards. Once the Dragonwand is with the statue, the destiny of the last dragon will unfold and all will be saved."

Markus laughed sarcastically. "So, this simple task is just to evade Royal Scouts, go into the infamous Dragon Citadel, find an ancient wand, bring it to the Capital, and present it to a statue?"

"Precisely" Tolen replied, mirroring Markus' sarcasm, which surprised the boy.

Markus sighed hard. "What about dragons at the Citadel? What if I'm caught?"

Tolen put his hand on Markus's arm. "I have faith in you, Markus of the Valley, or I would never have sent you the call. You are good enough to evade the foolish Guards that help the King, and there haven't been any dragons in Gallenor since the end of the War. You can do this. I know it. Without you, all is lost."

"How will I be allowed to study magic if I'm to go against the King? Why I should trust you? *You* might be the evil one, sending me to find the wand."

"I know you dream of dark wars. I know because I have seen them. The evil that is coming has turned your dreams dark. I have tried to help, to keep you from being traumatized, but I was not able to stop it all."

Markus realized that, in all of his dark dreams, something had come to rescue him, to keep him from being harmed. "It was *you* in my dreams?"

"Yes."

"Why?"

Tolen managed a smile and carefully took Markus by the hand. "You are a child, an innocent person who has only worried about the struggle of growing up. I needed you to be my champion and successor, but I also cared about your well-being. I am no villain trying to use you; I only ask what is necessary, because I know what true strength lies hidden in you. I do not have much strength left; my life is almost spent. I must know that you accept this journey, or I will die in vain, and all of Gallenor will be lost."

Markus looked at the old man and gave his words a lot of thought. He knew in his heart this wizard would not ask such a thing of him if it were not of the utmost importance. He had two paths to choose from: the path home or the path to a bigger life. Swallowing his fear and concerns, he nodded. "I accept."

"Good. You will do great things, young Markus of the Valley."

Markus smiled, his stomach feeling a little queasy and his body shaking at the prospect of journeying alone toward the unknown. "Do you have a map, book, or something to help me find my way?"

"The wand I gave you. Use it and you will learn secrets of the past. But remember, the only place to start is the beginning."

Markus frowned. "What does that mean?"

Tolen was about to answer, but the pounding of hooves rumbled outside. He looked up with real worry in his eyes. "Take the wand, and I will hide you from the Guards."

"Guards? Hide . . . what?"

"Now, or you will die under the blade of the King!" Tolen managed enough strength to yell, but he was fading fast.

Markus held out his hand and thought of the wand. It appeared in his palm, and then Tolen pointed a finger at the wand and said something so faint, Markus could not hear it. Suddenly, Markus saw the room through a blue haze. He was invisible to the rest of the world. The wand in his hands cast the spell, and as long as he held it and concentrated on the notion of invisibility, he would remain unseen.

"Tolen, we've found you! Come out, or we will break this door down!" the deep, commanding voice of the Captain of the Guards called out.

"Come, fool," Tolen commanded, and the door opened.

In walked a Guard in shining silver armor. Captain Morris of Thendor was famous around Gallenor; not just for his rank and fierce devotion to the throne, but for his dashing smile, piercing blue eyes, toned body, and confident swagger. He was a human and the highest ranked military commander under the King. With him were two other Guards, each holding his sword in readiness for whatever the wizard had waiting for them.

Captain Morris looked around, batted a few dangling things out of his way, and found the location of the wanted wizard. Stomping across the wooden floor with his heavy metal boots, he came right up to the bed and glared at the ancient man. "Tolen, it's time for you to come with us."

Tolen smiled feebly. "I would be happy to oblige your orders, Captain, but as you can see, I am near death. You will have to be satisfied in observing my final breaths."

Morris glowered at him. "No tricks, old man. We won't abandon our duty simply because you're attempting to distract us. Come, the King summons you for justice."

"Your foolishness knows no bounds, Morris. I have no strength left to lift myself, and in mere moments, I will no longer be with you. Report this to your King. Report that I, Tolen the Wise, have perished under the enemy of old age. My spells, and studies of what you call forbidden, are done. My search is finished. Farewell, young

Morris. May your kingdom strive to rise above fools such as you and your King."

"You are the fool, old man. Your plans have failed, and now I'm here to see that you're brought to justice."

Tolen turned his head and looked directly at Markus, though Morris believed himself to be the object of Tolen's sight. "My goals are yet realized. Once the Dragonwand is in the correct hands, your King's persecution of the wizards will be no more."

Morris sneered at Tolen. "Your pompous words will do you no good, old man. Prepare yourself. We will take you if we have to carry you."

"Carry me, then, for you will carry a dead body all the way back to your King." And, laughing softly, Tolen faded into death.

Morris shook the dead body. "Tolen . . . Tolen, no trickery!"

"Sir, I believe he's dead," one of the younger officers said as he approached the angered Captain.

Morris stopped shaking Tolen's body and looked around. "Don't let him deceive you. This old wizard has pulled many spells over our eyes these past five years."

"What do you want then, sir?" The Lieutenant waited for orders.

Morris snarled one last time at Tolen. "Stand guard around the house. I'll report to the King. If anything happens—*anything*—

report immediately."

"Understood, sir." The Lieutenant nodded.

Captain Morris began to walk out when he heard something odd. A rattling sound out of nowhere gave him pause. He walked toward the corner in which Markus waited and stopped for a second to listen.

Markus was so scared, he was shaking, and the little marble held in the wire on the top of the wand rattled against the metal. Slowly, he moved the wand closer to him and pressed it up against his chest, in hopes of stopping the sound.

"Sir?" the Lieutenant asked, breaking the silence.

Morris stood up straight to walk out again. "I just thought I heard something odd. Tight nerves on my part. Take your positions and be vigilant. I'll leave immediately."

"Yes, sir." The junior officer left with his Captain and commanded the other Guard to take up a position at the far end of the house. They would watch the house as long as their Captain commanded them to.

Captain Morris mounted his horse and galloped away for the castle in Thendor.

What now? Markus thought to himself. For a few moments, he waited and watched Tolen in hopes that the old wizard was, in fact, using some sort of magic to appear dead. But the old man simply lay in the eternal slumber. There was a slight smile on his face, as though he had won his final argument and everything was going to turn out well. That was easy for *him* to smile about. *He* wasn't the one being sent on a mission without many tools to accomplish it.

Markus had to get out of the house and away from the guards— that was obvious. He slowly walked through the house, each footstep taken so carefully that he hardly made a sound. When the floor squeaked even in the slightest, he lifted his foot and stepped somewhere else. It took quite some time, but he finally made it to the door. He could see both Guards from the windows and, to be safe, waited until the right time when both Guards had walked far enough away. He opened the door, slipped out, and closed it without making a sound. One step after another, he walked down the three stone steps and placed a careful foot onto the grass.

He was terribly proud of himself, right up until he heard a distinct *crunch*. Markus gasped and then held his breath. He looked down, seeing that his foot had landed on a small pile of large, dry leaves.

Both Guards turned and looked at each other. Markus hoped they would decide the other had made the sound, but they didn't. With furrowed brows and curious eyes, they came to investigate. Markus continued to hold his breath and stood perfectly still. They approached, each getting so close to him, he could feel their breath on his skin. They looked down to the leaves, not realizing that the squashed leaves that had made the sound were still under Markus's foot.

If Markus was visible, he would have been blue. The lack of oxygen made his head go woozy and his stomach a little queasy. After what seemed like hours of staring, both men peered around once more, looking for a squirrel or rabbit that might have made the noise.

"Must have been a nut," the Lieutenant declared and nodded to his fellow officer.

As they walked back to their posts, Markus took the opportunity to flee. Their feet were making just as many crunches as his. He was finally away from the cottage and ran as best he could into the trees. Once he felt his noises would not get their attention, he hit the ground on his knees and gasped in air. He hadn't even considered that he might have been able to breathe while running away; he was just too scared. It hurt to breathe, and he was lying on the ground, feeling like a boulder had dropped on him.

Looking at his hand, he realized he was no longer invisible. When he had finally come to a stop and lost focus on everything but getting some air, he had lost control of the spell. He waved the wand and tried to make himself invisible again, but it was not possible.

Whatever Tolen had done, Markus was not able to do without knowing the words or instructions. It would be nice to turn invisible now and then, but he would have to find that spell later. For now, he was just going to lie down and gather himself.

CHAPTER 2: DIVING RIGHT IN

MARKUS walked for two more days, pondering how he might finish his mission for the great wizard. Should he go back home and get help from his family and friends? *No*, he thought. His father would be angry with him for even taking such a dangerous mission.

"Dang it, old man! Why me?" He looked at the wand. "What do I do?" Then he had an idea. In one of his dreams, he was able to fly and go to faraway places using a spell. Perhaps, if he tried, he could get to the Dragon Citadel quickly. *What was that word?* The spell only had one word. Finally, he remembered. He held the wand up and said, "Fjuka!"

The marble on the top of the wand flashed brightly, and Markus lifted slowly into the air. A breeze wrapped around him and carried him up and up. For a moment, and only a very brief moment, he was amazed and marveled by the feeling of flight. Then, the spell took off. Markus blasted forward as though the wand was directing his path. To where, he really didn't know; he was too busy being thrown about like a leaf in a storm.

Left and right, the wand guided him through the forest, dragging him through the air. He barely missed three trees and came dangerously close to crashing into a large boulder before he flew right over the mountain. Looking out, he saw the Great Plains, tall mountains to the north, and distant oceans of the west of Gallenor. It was beautiful, exquisite, and the most amazing thing he had ever seen. He would have admired it more had he not looked down and realized he was being taken higher and higher into the breeze.

"Okay . . . uh . . . YAHH!" he shouted.

While considering his next move, he hit turbulence. The wand seemed to understand his need to land and directed him toward the ground. With his hand firmly gripped around the wand, Markus was tossed to and fro in the winds, while the ground quickly approached. This was bad. He just might have sealed his own fate with his first attempt to help Tolen.

Below, he saw a large body of water—a small lake or huge pond. It might have been enough to break his fall. But how could he maneuver himself toward it? The wand appeared to hear his thoughts, and it turned his descent towards the water. He hit the surface with a hard smack, skipped a few times like a flat stone, and then skidded right into a deeper part where he immediately sank. The wand had flown clear of his hand and vanished.

Markus was hurt and sinking fast. He looked up to see the light above him and started to swim to the surface. It was a burdensome challenge with what felt like a broken arm.

"What was that?!" he thought. Something had just shot into the

water, then another. Arrows! Someone was shooting at him!

Cresting the water and gasping in a harsh breath, Markus saw that two Dogkinds were aiming arrows at him from the shore. The Dog People of the Blue Forests were expert marksmen and would not miss, unless that was what they intended.

"Get out of our waters, imp!" a female voice yelled at him.

Markus continued to breathe hard and struggled to keep himself afloat. Moving was even harder, since he only had one good arm. "I . . . I can't! I need help!" he garbled out as loud as he could while the water began to envelope him, the pain in his arm too great to hold himself up.

The canine woman with light brown fur looked at the male next to her. "He may not be an imp. Rescue him before he drowns," she commanded, and the male Dogkind dropped his bow and jumped into the water.

After a swift swim and quick rescue, his hero laid Markus on the shore. He coughed while doing his best not to show he was in pain. "Thank you, whoever you are," he said weakly. Then he heard the stretching sound of a bow and an arrow being readied. He looked up to see the point of it directed at his face.

The dog woman flashed her fangs. "What sort of being are you?"

"Human," Markus quickly stated while holding his good arm up in defense.

She glared at him and then released the arrow. It struck the ground right next to his head. He had actually felt the shaft of the arrow brushing up against his ear.

"What are you doing?!" Markus tried to scoot away from her, but his broken arm prevented the escape. "Ow, ow, ow!"

She lowered her bow and leaned over to look at him. "If you were Impkind, you would have transformed back and flown away."

His eyes bugged. "Imp! You thought I was an imp?!"

The male Dogkind held out his hand to help Markus up. "We've been tracking a rogue imp through these trees for a week now. It has played many devious tricks on us to lull us into a false sense of security."

"I can assure you that I'm no imp. I'm human—and in a lot of pain." Markus rose to his feet and held his broken arm.

The male Dogkind looked at Markus's arm and then nodded toward the trees. "Come with us. Our healer can mend that easily."

"Thanks. Where do you live?" Markus asked.

"These forests are our home," the male replied.

"So, what's your name? I'm Markus of the Valley."

The male Dogkind answered, "I'm Treb, and this is my wife,

Kiin." Treb noticed that Markus was getting a good look at his wife's backside, her tail in particular. "Have you not seen my kind before?"

Markus looked up, embarrassed at having stared at Treb's wife. "No, in fact, I have not. I know of your people, however. You're Dogkind."

Kiin shot Markus a glare. "That is the human name for us. We are the Rakki." She was proud of this title and made sure he knew it.

"Rakki it is, then," Markus affirmed. A glow of green light caught the corner of his eye and he looked just in time to see it coming. "Watch out!"

Treb grabbed Markus and pushed him out of the way, just as the bolt of energy blasted the ground near them. Both Rakki grabbed their bows and notched arrows, ready to fire. Flying around was a small, demon-like creature with bat wings. It was an imp—a mischievous pest that had no feelings for what it destroyed.

Kiin launched arrow after arrow at the little monster, only to miss. She was good, but the imp was faster and could evade her with ease. Cackling, the imp lobbed more energy balls. With a well-placed shot, it threw Kiin across the ground and partly into the water. She was out cold, but still breathing. Then it turned its sights toward Markus.

Without hesitation, Markus held out his hand and said, "Wand!"

It appeared on command. He logrolled to the side, dodging a green energy blast and yelled, "Eldr!" The wand produced an impressive ball of fire destroying the next incoming energy attack, and continued on to blast the imp out of the air.

When the little creature hit the ground, Treb sent one last arrow at it, piercing it through. Within seconds, the imp exploded in a flash of green.

Markus sat for a second, shocked by his own power. He had never created a spell that well and that powerful before.

"Kiin!" Treb ran over to his wife and found her on the ground, out cold.

Markus got up and quickly joined him. "Is she okay?"

Treb looked her over, sniffing her with his nose. "I don't know. She's still breathing and does not look hurt, but she won't wake. Damned imp spells."

"What can we do?"

Treb looked at Markus and then at the wand. "You're a wizard. Can't you do something?"

Markus shook his head and stepped back. "No, I . . . I'm not a real wizard. I'm not even an apprentice."

"Come, we have to return to the village. The healers can help." Treb gently picked up his wife and carried her in his arms.

Markus took up Kiin's bow and carried it as he followed right behind them.

Within the walls of Thendor, the Capital of Gallenor, was a large courtyard that had a single statue in it. It was a three-story-tall dragon, appearing as though it was still in the throes of battle. The statue had not been created by just any artisan; it had actually been a real dragon centuries ago. The last known dragon during the Great War had been mysteriously turned to stone. The head wizard under the first King had explained that the dragon was dangerous and should be feared.

For centuries, the people of Gallenor ignored it, but never forgot the threat the dragon had once posed. Should it return to life, all the people of Gallenor would be in danger. The current head wizard under King Anthony discovered that the statue was, in fact, the real form of the Head of the Wizardry College. Tolen the Wise, who was known to be an Ancient, was actually the last dragon. He had found a way to separate himself from the statue to live as a man all those years.

Tolen had denied the allegation, but the facts proved him to be a liar. Hallond, the head wizard, explained that the seal that kept the dragon at bay was breaking, and when it broke completely, the dragon would return. The only hope of stopping it would be to find the Dragonwand, the instrument all dragon wizards used to perform their most powerful spells. With it, they could destroy the statue and secure peace.

At that moment, King Anthony and the court wizards approached the dragon statue. The elderly king sat atop a beautiful white horse and anxiously waited good news. Though the dragon statue was within the walls of Thendor, the area around it was given a wide berth and no buildings had ever been built close by. The only reason the wall was built around it was so the statue would always be under the watchful eye of the Royal Guard.

The Captain of the Guard, Morris, approached and knelt down on one knee before the King. "Your Highness, the guards have reported in. Tolen is truly dead. We were unable to locate his Dragonwand. It must have died with him."

The King, an old man with a white beard, dressed purple robes lined in gold, nodded to his loyal Captain. "Then everything is as it should be. The last ancient wizard has passed, and this statue can finally be destroyed."

"If that is your command." Morris awaited the final order.

With another nod, the King gave the command. "Court wizards, do your duty!"

Fifteen wizards approached the huge dragon statue, and each

produced a single ball of fire. In unison, they proceeded to destroy the statue. A great and powerful fireball encompassed the stone beast, yet the dragon was unscathed. It remained standing, its claws still out, maw open, and eyes fixed upon the palace.

"What is this?!" the King demanded, furious.

The head wizard approached the King and knelt down. "Your Majesty, the protection spell around the statue is still in place. We cannot destroy it. There must be an active Dragonwand in this world, or the spell would break."

The King let out a disappointed sigh. "Captain Morris, set up a garrison around this statue to protect it from being touched by that wand. Then prepare your finest legion and scour the kingdom for that Dragonwand."

"As you command, Your Majesty."

Markus was led into an amazing city hidden within the forest. Homes, shops, and other buildings were built among the trees. Some were on the ground, while others were high in the branches. A massive system of rope bridges connected the structures and created a web-like appearance.

Treb carried his wife through the city to a hut. Inside were the healers: an old man and his daughter, as well as another young girl.

The youngest was about Markus' age and very shy when she first met the human. Her name was Crystal, and she had something in common with Markus. She could use a little magic.

Markus sat in the hut and watched the old man and his daughter tend to Kiin. They used some talismans to disenchant the spell the imp had placed on Kiin. It was not hurting her, other than keeping her from waking. Neither the old man nor his daughter were able to use magic, but they were brilliant with healing herbs and potions. They were well trained with the talismans they had obtained from real wizards.

Crystal looked at Markus' arm, feeling up and down the magically mended bone to be certain her spell had worked. She looked like all the other Rakki he had met. All over her body was thick, light brown fur. She had a fluffy, reddish brown tail with a white tip like a fox's. Her ears were set a little higher on her head than a human's, and were tall with the fur creating points at the ends. Her hands and feet were shaped like a human's, as were all the Rakkis, which surprised Markus. He had imagined they would look more animal-like in their appendages.

Her face, though, had a touch of canine to it. The upper lip was puffier with some whiskers growing out on either side. The nose was cold, dark, and wet. Her eyes were brilliantly blue—the reason she was named Crystal—and they shone like gems. Markus found her attractive, more so than he thought he would a furry dog-woman. Unlike Treb and Kiin, who both wore a unique Rakki armor, the rest wore very simple clothing. Their clothes were not unlike what everyone else wore, but had allowances for their tails.

"Your arm—it's healed," she said.

He held up his arm and felt it. "Oh, thanks. Where did you learn your magic?"

"I taught myself."

This highly intrigued him. "Really! How?"

"Rakki are lore keepers. We have a vast library from all over the known world. We have a few old spell books. I've been studying them."

Markus, doing his best to be charming, grinned and asked, "Can you show me this library?"

Crystal shyly returned his flirty smile. "I can take you there. But you must wait until tomorrow. The library does not have its doors open after dark."

Markus was very eager. "Okay. Then, when can we go?"

"Tomorrow morning." Crystal stood up and closed the little notebook she kept her spells written in.

"Oh, well, I was hoping to get going by tomorrow. I have an

important mission, and I just need to see if your library has a map. Though, looking at a spell book or two could be fun."

Crystal turned around, the same shy smile on her face. "We Rakki have a saying, 'Chase tomorrow and you lose today.' Why don't you spend the evening here with us and learn more about our kind? I would love to know more about you and your amazing wand."

Markus frowned. He had not had his wand out since he came into the village. "How did you know about it?"

"Treb's my father. He told me about your wand."

Markus had not expected to hear that. "Treb's your father? I didn't think he would be old enough to have a daughter your age."

"It's a long story. Perhaps I'll tell it to you over dinner. You do eat food, Humankind?"

"It's just *human*, though you may call me Markus. And, yes, I do eat food. I could use some right about now. I haven't eaten since I arrived nine hours ago." He got up off of the bed he had been sitting on. With another flirty smile he said, "After dinner, maybe you could show me around. Tell me more about this place, about you." He slipped the last part in quickly.

She blushed under her fur. "Sounds like fun."

Crystal walked with him toward the door. He stopped where Treb was sitting next to Kiin's bed and patted the burly Rakki's shoulder. "Thanks for saving me."

Treb forced a smile. "Sure."

"Will she be okay?"

"She's a strong warrior. This isn't the first imp we've battled, and it won't be the last."

"Glad to hear that." Markus continued out with Crystal at his side. He noted that Treb was sort of giving him the stink eye just before the cloth door shut behind them. What had he done?

CHAPTER 3: UNEXPECTED DISCOVERIES

"THAT was good. I haven't had chicken made like that before. It was really . . . spicy." Markus was still cooling his mouth from the heat of the spices used in the dish Crystal had just served. He would've preferred it to not be so spicy, but he didn't want to offend her.

She laughed at him as she listened to him breathe a little heavier to cool off his tongue. "Rakki love hot food. The spicier the better."

Markus hung his tongue out a little and practically panted, which drew even more eyes on him from the passing people. Fortunately, it was not an insulting gesture, but awkward.

Crystal had decided to take him on a stroll through the trees to show him her village. She was proud of her home and it showed. While she was a shy, quiet person when he first met her, she beamed with pride when she spoke about the Rakki's village and their accomplishments.

"So, are there any other Rakki villages around Gallenor?" Markus asked.

Crystal nodded. "A few. None this large, but all inside forests. My kind enjoys being around the trees."

Markus noted the multitude of small farms inside the city that were populated with many chickens. "I see that poultry seems to be popular among your kind."

"Oh, yes. Chickens, ducks, geese—all kinds. Fowl makes up most of our meat. Do the Humankind eat a lot of birds?"

"Yes, but not quite as much as the Rakki. We eat a lot of vegetables and fruits. In fact, where I am from is a large farming community that mostly grows fruits and grains."

"Do you not have much food other than plants?"

"The Lizardkind that live outside of the main villages raise pigs, cows, ducks, and goats. So, we get meat, though most of the animals are raised primarily for what they produce. Milk, eggs, manure."

She shuddered. "I can't imagine eating just plants." Brushing it off, she asked, "Did you use your magic to help the farmers?"

"No." He laughed at the thought. "In fact, I was sort of an embarrassment to my family. I was supposed to inherit the farm, just like my father and grandfather. So, I grew up in the dirt."

"Your people did not encourage your craft?" It was a stunning revelation to her.

"Not really. I'm from a simple farming community. You do what is expected of you." He kicked at the ground a little. "It didn't help that I learned just enough magic to be a menace."

"Huh?"

He laughed at himself, considering how foolish he had been. "I found an old book that had some spells in it. I tried to learn how to use them. I set more than one fire and caused a few sonic booms. Nothing was ever destroyed, and I did no real harm, but I scared people. Wizards haven't been seen in the valley for decades. So, to those old farmers, magic is scary."

"To the unwise, magic can appear dangerous and frightening. I know some of our own are scared by my abilities. But, my ambition is to be a healer, so I never set any fires or created booms."

"You're lucky you have been able to train."

She frowned at him. "But, you now have a powerful wand? Father said you cast a huge fireball at the imp and helped stop it. Surely, only a wizard would have a wand like yours."

"An old wizard gave it to me, along with a mission to follow, after he passed on. The wand is powerful, but I am not a real wizard yet. I am not even an apprentice. You're better at this than I."

She laughed and shook her head. "I am a mere novice, not a real wizard yet. I wish I could learn more about magic, but it is forbidden."

Her admission caught his attention right away. "Forbidden? What about the college?"

"Don't you know? The Royal Guards have been rounding up wizards for years. Magic lessons have been banned and the college closed. My parents were taken four years ago, and I've not seen them since."

"I guess that's what Tolen was referring to when he told me the King was paranoid about magic and wizards. I didn't realize how bad it was." Suddenly, he realized something else she had said. "Wait a minute." Markus stopped walking. "Your parents? I thought Treb and Kiin . . ."

"They're good friends of my family. When my mother and father were taken, they took me in."

Markus was still in shock and began to become angry. "Have you not thought about going after them? Freeing them?"

"I want to go and find them. Many nights, I've dreamed of sneaking into the prison and setting them free. But, I was a little girl when they were taken from me. I cannot go alone."

"What about the rest of the Rakki? Are they all right with this ludicrous order? If anyone invaded the valley and stole people, I'm sure my friends would—"

Crystal stopped him. "With what?"

"Huh?"

"The Royal Army is large and powerful. If we went in to get back

47

our kinfolk, they would crush us in an afternoon." She looked like she was about to cry.

Markus took her hand and held it. "I'm sorry. I didn't mean to make you sad."

She mustered a smile and looked him in the eye. "It's all right. I know you didn't mean anything bad by it. You simply don't understand."

"No, I'm afraid I don't. Wizards don't come around the valley much. My family members were about the only ones still left in the valley who could use magic, but they never trained or practiced, so I guess we were ignored when this gathering of wizards happened. The only wizard left was Tolen, and he had been evading the Royals . . . apparently."

She let go of his hand and sat down on a bench. "It was an awful night. A legion of the Royal Army, led by this tall Humankind in fancy armor, came and asked to speak with our leader. Everyone was worried about what was happening. I was so scared. I heard people mention war, dragon attacks, and many other terrible things."

Markus sat next to her. "When did they take them?"

Her lip quivered, but she forced herself not to cry. Gulping in a breath, she continued, "The Rakki couriers came to each home of the known wizards and announced they were to surrender themselves to the King at Thendor for the good of the kingdom. I didn't understand. I only knew they were taking away my family. My father came to me and fell on his knees. He put his arms around me and held me so close, I could feel his heart beating. My mother put her arms around both of us, and they cried. I had never seen tears in my father's eyes before. Then, they told me to conceal my abilities and not to tell anyone for at least a year I was able to use magic. My father and mother walked me over to Treb and Kiin's home and asked them to watch over me until they returned. Mom told me to respect Treb and Kiin as I would my own parents. Then . . ." She paused to collect herself. "Then, they told me they loved me and would return. With that, they surrendered themselves to the Royal Guards and were taken away with the rest of the wizards."

Markus put his arm around her. "I'm so sorry. My mom and dad frustrate me some days, but I can't imagine watching them be taken away as prisoners."

"Of all the wizard families in our village, I was the only child that could use magic. I waited a year for them to come back, hiding my abilities. Once we were sure the Royals were not looking for wizards among our kind any longer, I began to study and taught myself magic. I would become a healer and make my mother and father proud once they returned. But . . . they haven't."

"Yet," he said, trying to be positive. "They haven't returned *yet*. They're still alive and . . . and you will see them soon."

"Really? How do you know?"

"Wand!" he called out, and his new wand appeared in his hand. "An ancient and powerful wizard gave me this wand and a mission. I'm to find a Dragonwand and return it to a statue. The Ancient said a darkness was coming to Gallenor, and my mission would protect us from the darkness. Once I'm done, I'm sure the wizards will be freed."

She was stunned. "Is this true?"

He smiled at her charmingly to revive the smile she had lost a while back. "I have no reason to lie."

Crystal giggled and looked into his eyes. It was probably him doing his best to flirt with her, or it could have been all this talk about seeing her family again, but she was beginning to really like this Humankind.

Markus asked, "I've heard you call Treb and Kiin your mother and father—why? Shouldn't you just call them by their names? They aren't your real parents."

"No, they aren't," Crystal affirmed. "But to me, they're my parents right now. I love and respect them as my mother and father. If they had any children of their own, those children would be my brothers and sisters. I show Treb and Kiin respect by calling them Mother and Father."

"That's sweet," Markus said, and then twirled his wand around. "Hey, I think I remember a fireworks spell. Wanna see me try?"

"A-HEM!" a voice interrupted, breaking up the little exchange of glances. Both children looked to see Treb standing before them, still in his armor, his muscular arms folded, and his eyes fixed on Markus. "What is going on here?" he demanded.

Crystal stood up while gently removing Markus' arm from around her shoulders. "My new friend was just telling me about his wand."

Treb, still glaring at Markus, asked, "Was that *all* he was doing?" The insinuation in his voice was unmistakable.

Crystal gasped, "Father! Don't be rude. He was just being friendly."

Treb gave Markus one last, over-protective-father look, and then turned. "Come, it's getting late, and Kiin needs a little help from your magic to sleep tonight."

Crystal waited a second for her father to move a few steps away. Once he was, she quietly said, "Thanks."

"For what?" Markus asked.

"For trying to give me hope. I had forgotten it was still in my heart, but it's right where I left it."

Markus restated an old line from a poem he had read once. "Hope is frail, but hard to kill."

"Rest well tonight. Tomorrow, I'll show you the library. It's quite something to see."

Treb yelled out when he noticed Crystal wasn't walking behind him. " Hey! Aren't you coming home tonight?!"

She smiled at Markus one last time. "Good night." With that, she turned and ran to catch up to her adoptive father.

Markus watched her walk away, her tail wagging. She was certainly cute, which was something he never imagined he would have thought about anyone with a tail.

Markus settled into his room at the inn. Treb and Kiin had kindly arranged for him to have a place to stay—a reward for him helping save them from the imp attack. He was happy to be sleeping on a soft bed and in a warm room. Since he had left home, he had been sleeping under the stars. That kind of life had its charm but lacked some of the comforts he was used to.

All throughout the evening, what Crystal had said to him played on his mind. Wizardry was outlawed? Why? Wizards were usually kind helpers who utilized their talents to enhance the lives of everyone. Markus wanted to use his magic to assist the farmers with their crops, and even protect the village from the infrequent bandit attacks. But that had all changed now. He was considered a fugitive just for having magical powers.

Sitting at a small table in the room, he pondered everything. This mission already had its difficulties, but now it was looking to be impossible. What if he was discovered? How was he supposed to find this Dragonwand, all by himself, in a land that now wanted to imprison him for being a wizard? Taking a deep breath, he realized how late it was and that he had to get some sleep. He would figure things out tomorrow.

After snuffing out the candles, Markus lay down on his bed. He smiled at the feeling of feathers beneath him. The mattress, pillows, and comforter were all stuffed with chicken feathers. Probably a by-product of all the chicken farms in the area. It was a much softer bed than what he had expected.

For well over two hours, he tried to sleep, but he couldn't. It wasn't the words Crystal had said to him, but his feelings that had stirred him. She had lost her parents in a terrible way, and missed them dearly. What if his mother and father were gone? He began to think of the day before he had left.

His mother had been angry as ever at him. She had expected all of her lectures about being a member of the family and tending their farm would have sunk in. His father wasn't as angry, but filled with disappointment. Both of his parents had spent the better part of the past year trying to control his life and tell him what his future would be. They both ignored his worries about his strange dreams. His father, a person who denied his own magical side, had said the dreams would go away when Markus finally gave up on his goal of learning about magic. But Markus had not been convinced.

From the time he was ten to the day he turned fifteen, he had apprenticed to Farmer Joel, a friend of the family. It was tradition that Markus would spend five years working in the field his father chose for him, but not on the family's field. Joel was a nice old man who raised strawberries and even a little silk grass, a plant used to spin into fabrics. Markus had planted, tended, and harvested like a good farmhand.

He wasn't half bad, which was to be expected, considering he had spent his life on a farm. But, in his down time, he practiced what little magic he could. At first, his father tried to teach him how to suppress magical abilities in the same ways that he had. But Markus wasn't going to hear of that. Magic wasn't a burden; it was a gift.

What surprised Markus the most was that Farmer Joel had encouraged him to learn magic. He was the oldest farmer in the valley and had known that wizards had used to help farmers. They could help heal ill cattle, remove swarms of bugs, and bring water during dry times. After a lifetime of struggling as a farmer, Markus finally realized he could help ease the struggles of his fellow farmers, especially his family. But they were still stubborn about their beliefs. He wasn't going to learn magic if they had their way.

A month before any boy turned sixteen, he was allowed to go out into the world and decide what he wanted to do with his life. It was an old tradition most children avoided, especially those sheltered in the old farm communities. Unlike the other children, Markus seemed to be born with ambition in his blood. He wanted to learn and grow, to see the world outside of the valley. This tradition allowed Markus to go the school of his choosing, and he chose to go to a Wizardry School. His mother and father were angry with him. They told him he was not allowed, but Markus found the town magistrate and affirmed that once he turned sixteen, he had the right to go to college. This only made the situation worse at home. His parents were now extremely determined to keep him home. The fights became so bad, it had nearly come to blows between him and his mother. His father hardly spoke to him. When his father *did* speak to him, it was all about keeping the family tradition alive, tend the farm . . . and nothing else.

The day before he set out was the worst day of his life with his parents. The screaming match got so bad that a family friend who had walked by their home ran to get the magistrate. She was certain the family was at each other's throats, and she was nearly correct.

When the magistrate arrived, he only found a heated family argument. However, he had told Markus' parents that they had no legal right to keep their son at home, though he had advised Markus to listen to them. It seemed everyone outside of Farmer Joel was against Markus leaving. But his teenage stubbornness wanted to prove them all wrong. He made up his mind, packed himself up, and left. He should've brought more with him, but he was ready to leave.

Considering all he knew now, he realized why the magistrate had encouraged Markus to learn how to suppress his magical side. Byron was a kind old man who had served the valley community for over twenty years. He had protected Markus from the wizard law. It was likely he had expected Markus to fail in finding a wizard to write him his letter, and that was why he hadn't stopped him from going. Now, Markus was out here, and there was so much against him, he almost wanted to go home . . . *almost.*

Looking back, Markus was still angry at his parent's attitude. But he was also a little worried. What if something happened to him? What if something happened to them? They might have been angry at each other, but he still loved them and knew perfectly well they loved him. He could go home right now and they would be there. Crystal did not have that option. She only had her memories and a vague hope. He wanted to tell his parents he was sorry. He wasn't sorry for believing in his abilities and his own future, but he was sorry for yelling at them. He was sorry for not telling them he loved them before he left. His heart ached. He had felt so grown-up since he left home, but right now, he felt like he was six years old.

For the rest of the night, he lay in bed and did his best to convince himself not to go home tomorrow. He still had a mission and would complete it. Once that was done, however, he would go home and make sure his parents were all right. This mission wouldn't take too long, and then all would be right. At least, that was the logic he used to sate his fears.

CHAPTER 4: COURTS AND WIZARDS

A young assistant walked alongside the King's personal wizard. They approached a large rock structure near the outskirts of the Capital.

The Pale Labyrinth was a place built to house wizards who were deemed too dangerous to be allowed to go free. It held thousands of people, each in an alcove of stone that was enchanted to put the person into a deep, permanent sleep. Over the centuries of its existence, the Pale Labyrinth was used for no more than one hundred wizards at a time. Now, it was pushed to its limits. Thousands of wizards rested in the space meant for far fewer, almost none of them guilty of anything but being born.

"Uh, sir, what happens if we find more wizards?" the assistant hesitantly asked.

Head Wizard Hallond touched a magical barrier that was placed in a doorway to the outside. It flashed against his touch, showing him it was still at full strength. The old man looked up at his fellow wizards in their deep slumber. "We can house fifteen more before the labyrinth becomes full."

"I know. What then, sir?"

"Then, young Horace, we will have to construct more alcoves and enchant them as these were. That is assuming we do not find a way to end the threat and finally release them."

Horace grimaced at the sight of all the other wizards held in the labyrinth. "It's awful to be locked away like that. Are we sure this is the only way?"

Hallond turned so the young man beside him could not see the smile on his face. Something about this place brought a touch of enjoyment to him. "It is the only way. Soon, I wager, their incarceration will be over and they will be free to go about their lives. Soon, this will finally come to an end, after so many years and so much planning, and it will all finally be just right."

Horace, a little confused by what his master was saying, asked, "Are you okay, sir?"

"I'm fine. Just looking forward to letting my friends go."

"Why can't we let them go now? Surely they aren't a danger to us, and I bet they could help us find the Dragonwand."

"It is the orders of the King that prevents their release until such a time as the wand is found, and King Anthony is a wise man. Now, let's get moving. We shouldn't be late. King Anthony is also impatient." He shooed along the young assistant so they could head for the Royal Court.

King Anthony's Royal Courtroom was a regal place with many fine and intricate tapestries hanging from the walls. Tall windows that let in an abundance of light and beautiful views of the land surrounding Thendor Province complimented the tall ceiling. The ceiling was held up with great pillars carved with the history of the kingdom since the War. Over a thousand years were chronicled into the carving of these pillars, and they were studied intensely by historians when the court was not in session.

At the front of the room was a large wooden chair inlaid with gold, bronze, and silver. The bronze was the base layer, covering the throne underneath the other embellishments. On top of it were large patches of silver that were embossed with geometric designs. Inside the designs were plates of pure gold, each holding a symbol, a crest of each king who sat upon this throne. King Anthony's crest was a flying phoenix—the symbol of heroism to the Kingdom of Gallenor.

At that very moment, the throne was occupied by His Majesty, King Anthony. His regal staff was in his right hand, and his eyes were glued to those around him. Surrounding him were his advisers, members of the voting council, and a few courtiers sent by the different provinces of Gallenor. The majority of the people present were human. There was one representative of the Shlan, or Lizardkind, a woman by the name of Hssovk. There was a Rakki, or

Dogkind, a man by the name of Norl. Last, there was a Momar, or Dwarfkind, present. His name was Jarl, and he was a very loud, grumpy, old man who rarely involved his people in anything of importance in Gallenor.

The only person not present, who should have been there, was Hallond, the Chief Wizard under the King. This was making the King displeased, but it did give the others present a moment to speak for their people.

Speaking currently was Hssovk, the Lizardkind representative. "My people are not happy about thissss. We demand you releassse our wizards." She was articulate for a Shlan, though none of the Lizardkind could work the hiss completely out of their speech.

King Anthony shook his head. "That is not possible right now. We are still dealing with the issue at hand."

Norl spoke up. "We've been without our wizards for four years now. How long is this going to take? When will we see the conclusion?"

Hssovk added, "They have rightssss too!" This started a bit of nasty murmuring among the people present.

The King banged the end of his staff on the ground, causing an unnaturally loud boom to rattle everyone in the room. Once they were quietly waiting on him, he spoke. "The situation will resolve itself when it resolves itself. We can no more force the issue than we already have. This is a dangerous state of affairs."

Charles, the local Provincial Governor, approached the throne. "Your Majesty, it's rumored the wizard Tolen has passed on. Shouldn't that herald the end of this?" Charles treated the King with extreme reverence, though his treatment was merely a ploy to gain influence from the King.

King Anthony nodded. "We will hear about that soon enough." Just then, to the relief of the King, the doors at the opposite end of the hall opened and in came Hallond and his young assistant. The wizard carried himself with dignity when he walked. He held a rank second only to the King himself.

The Chief Wizard approached the throne and knelt down. "Your Majesty." His assistant, Horrace, did the same but did not speak.

King Anthony waved his hand. "Rise, my old friend, and report."

Hallond stood up and looked around the room. "The guards tell the truth. Tolen the Wise is no longer living. His body has been burned, and his home was destroyed only this morning."

Those in the room began to ask questions at once: "Doesn't this mean it's over?" "What about the Dragonwand?" "Who killed him?"

Hallond held up his hands. "Please, there is more." But he couldn't get them to stop their queries.

The King banged his staff again. "Silence!" The action brought the questions to a dead stop. Then King Anthony addressed Hallond. "What of the statue?"

Hallond pulled out a large flask of water and poured all of it out. As it fell from the mouth of the bottle, it floated in the air. The water swirled around until it formed a clear disc, hovering in the middle of the room. Once that was done, Hallond walked around it with his wand held out. "Sja Asferd, dyr!"

When he spoke, the wand produced a glowing gold powder that swirled about in the water's surface. The gold powder gathered in several locations and began to glow brightly, some places more than others. He stopped walking and looked closely at one particular glowing mass of gold. Rubbing his white beard, he pondered the pool for a while. Everyone else in the room was dead silent, waiting on him to say something.

"Hallond?" King Anthony broke the silence.

Hallond turned to the King and, with a sorrowful brow, said, "The power within the statue still grows. Its seal is still breaking." Gasps and murmurs erupted from the attending crowd.

King Anthony stood up and walked over to the hovering pool. He looked into it, the glowing golden hues dancing in his eyes. "How long?"

"A matter of weeks at best, maybe even days."

Hssovk asked, "What could it be? Who issss doing thisss?"

Norl was agitated. "I thought you said locking up all of our wizards would put a stop to this!"

Omar of Glenoth added, "The wizard Tolen was the last known ancient wizard, and he's dead! What do we do now?"

Hssovk glared at Hallond. "What of them? What of the court'ssss own wizardsss?"

Jarl, the dwarf, grumbled in his thick dwarven brogue, "What if it tis ah ploy? What if the wizards under the king be manipulatin' us all?"

King Anthony would hear none of this. He turned to them and silenced them with a single look. Once he had their undivided attention, he set them straight. "The court wizards are the only ones standing between the dragon's return and your destruction. I will not hear of this dissension."

Hssovk asked, "What then? What do we do now?"

King Anthony returned to his throne and sat back down. "The only answer is there is an unknown element. Someone or something we have overlooked."

Norl frowned. "That's terribly vague."

"I'm aware of that!" The King grew annoyed that they always expected him to have all the answers. His advisers seemed more worried about making accusations than considering the options. So, he looked upon the one man who he trusted the most. "Wizard Hallond, what say you?"

Hallond had his flask out and was bringing the water back into it. After it was full, he corked it and turned to the audience. "There must be another player in this. Someone who is helping Tolen finish his work."

"Who could do this? Aren't all the wizards accounted for yet?" a courtier asked.

"Only three . . ." Horace spoke up, and then just about swallowed his words when everyone, including the King, stared at him. He cleared his throat and continued. "Only three wizards escaped the school and were not accounted for."

Hallond smiled at his nervous assistant and nodded in agreement. "We presumed the rogue wizard professors were killed while fleeing, but we did not account for their bodies. It isn't impossible they are still out there, for I cannot imagine anyone with less power and skill than a school wizard could keep up Tolen's evil work. This person, or persons, must be stopped at all costs."

King Anthony nodded in agreement. "Then it shall be. The Guards will be sent out and ordered to scour the land once again.

We will stop this menace before it's too late. Representatives, return to your people and tell them to expect the Guards to be in their lands. They are to give them passage without hindrance. They will obey them, as the Royal Guard will be under orders of the Throne."

The crowd all nodded, one at a time, in agreement. Most did not seem to be pleased, but they knew it was their duty to follow the King's orders.

Outside the court, Hssovk and Norl spoke. It was an odd sight, for the Lizardkind and Dogkind had never gotten along well. But, that aside, they were speaking amicably.

Norl whispered to his fellow courtier, "Do you trust Hallond?"

Hssovk looked around to see that no prying eyes were on them. "No. Thisss is ssstarting to look more and more ssusspiciouss to my people."

"What of the Guards? They will be scouting our lands again, unnerving our people and possibly stealing more of our kin." Norl was leery of the King's orders.

"I cannot deny the King'sss order. But I do not have to like it." She looked around one more time. "If the Rakki were to stage an uprissssing against thiss, the Sssshaln would be at your side."

Norl shook his head, a touch of a smile on his face. "We're not ready to declare a coup against the King. Besides, would my people even believe me if I told them of your offer?"

Hssovk smiled her thin lizard lips. "No, I sssupose not. Travel well, my friend." She bid him farewell and left to head to her embassy in Thendor to prepare for her long journey home.

The Rakki representative decided he might address the King in person, in private. His people had been asking him for almost a year now to negotiate the return of their wizards from the Pale Labyrinth. He would be returning home soon, and he wanted to at least go back with the knowledge that he had tried everything he could.

Norl approached the throne and asked the Chief of the Palace Guard for an audience with the King, as procedure dictated that the Chief must escort any who ask for an audience. Chief Alex quickly agreed and walked Norl back toward the King's personal chambers. Few courtiers were more respected or well known as Norl of the Rakki. He was wise, calm, humble, and, above all, intelligent. The Palace Guards held him in high regard and would often give him allowances not granted to others. In fact, Norl was escorted to the King's chambers. It was not customary for anyone to stand there to wait. If the King was speaking with anyone else, the person waiting was usually asked to wait by the throne until called upon. Not even the Guards stood so near the King's chamber doors, but Norl posed no threat to security, and surely the King wouldn't mind.

The dog man stood there quietly. Being a courtier meant a lot of waiting and patience, which Norl demonstrated often. As a Rakki, he had superior hearing over most humans or any of the other races. Right then, this keen hearing picked up on the conversation within the King's chambers all too well. The King was speaking with Wizard Hallond. Norl attempted to ignore the conversation for their benefit, but their words drew his attention.

"Do you think we can keep them at bay for much longer?" the King asked Hallond.

The wizard responded coolly, "Yes. By the time they finally realize what is truly happening, it will be far too late."

"The Shlan ambassador was in to see me a day ago about freeing her people, and I'm sure the others will not be far behind. Keeping up the pretense about the wizards is not easy," the King lamented.

Hallond calmly replied, "History supports our story. Wizards did dark deeds during the War. If it had not been for the dragons, the dark wizards could have taken control of everything."

"Are you sure this will work?" the King asked the question as though he had asked it many times before.

"As sure as I am a wizard. Once we have the Dragonwand and can finally destroy that horrible statue, my real students will be able to put to rest all the pathetic leaders of the people and make you supreme lord of all. Then, with the combined magic of all the prisoners, I can finalize the spell that will grant you and all my followers immortality."

"What of Tolen's plans?"

Hallond's response was quick and sharp. "Tolen is dead, and with him died any possible resistance. I have waited for over a thousand years for that old fool to die. I cannot say I did not try to help him along a few times. How amazing that time itself finally did him in."

"The dragon statue still stands and keeps your powers at bay. Tolen's statue should be dead if he is dead!" The King was angry.

"Rest assured, My Lord, the statue's seal over me and my followers is waning quickly. Once we have the Dragonwand in our possession, the statue will be rubble and a new age of Gallenor will rise."

The King let out a tired sigh. "I don't know, Hallond. I'm still having second thoughts about all of this."

Hallond put on the convincing tone that politicians attain for such situations as the present. "Sire, you must not let those foolish ideas enter your head. We are too far along with this to have second thoughts. Besides, we are doing this for the good of the kingdom."

"I know. But, it is just so many lies. We have told the people of

69

Gallenor nothing but lies for years now."

Hallond comforted the King. "Is it not the duty of every citizen of Gallenor to work for a better tomorrow?"

"Well, yes," the King answered.

"You have no heir, and, pardon me, but at your age, you are unlikely to produce an heir. So, my plan is the best thing for our future. You will be granted immortality, along with a few others with real power. Gallenor will have a leadership that will not age or die, and a brighter future will be ahead. All it will cost are the lives of a few loyal citizens of Gallenor."

"Do we have to kill all of the wizards for this?" When the King said this, Norl whimpered a little outside the door, but it did not draw attention to him. The Rakki quickly covered his mouth and though his tail was between his legs, he stayed to keep listening. He had to hear this.

"I am afraid that it has to be." Realizing the King was in need of more convincing, Hallond asked a leading question. "Would you not ask your soldiers to die for Gallenor?"

"Of course. But, this is different."

"I don't see how. Do not worry. In time, the brilliance of this will truly sink in. Once you are granted immortality, all the answers will be made perfectly clear. Trust me."

The King asked the question that was on Norl's mind. "Won't the people resist this once they find out the truth?"

Hallond calmly answered, "Have faith in me, Sire. All will work out according to my plans." He paused and then said, "I think I hear someone."

Norl's ears perked up and he started to step back. When he realized Hallond was approaching the door, he bolted. Hallond opened the door to find exactly what he hoped: nothing. So, he returned to the King, after making sure the door was securely closed.

Standing on the other side of a square column, Norl's heart was pounding and his breath was trembling. In all his years of service to Gallenor and his people, he had never expected to hear such hideous things. A deep part of him begged for it to be a dream—a terrible, horrible dream. But, the reality was that it was no dream and he had to tell someone. But who could he trust? He had to go home. He had to bring this to his own leaders. The head of the Rakki people was a wise and honorable man. He would know what to do next.

CHAPTER 5: BOOKS

MARKUS woke early. Although he had gone to sleep much later than usual, his dreams were a bit darker than normal, and it seemed his mind wanted out. It was nice to wake up in a warm room, on a soft bed. However, the moment he woke up, his mind returned to the worries from the night before. He thought about his parents and his journey. Was he really ready for this? Could he do it alone? What if he were stopped, or even placed in the prison where they were keeping Crystal's parents? He wanted to find courage somewhere so he could push onward. He knew he might be the last one standing between a dark day and the freedom of all magic users in Gallenor. But why him? He was only fifteen. Yes, he was going to turn sixteen in a few days, but that made very little difference.

Suddenly, his thoughts were broken by the sound of a soft knock on his door. "Markus, are you awake yet?" It was the gentle voice of Crystal.

He brightened up, smiled, and answered the door. There she stood with a kind smile and a nervous posture.

"Uh, good morning, Markus. Did you sleep well?"

Markus grinned at her and nodded. "Yes. Anything is better than on the cold hard ground." He could see her fighting a smile and holding in a chuckle. "What is it?"

She pointed to his bare chest because he was only wearing his pants. "I have never seen so little fur." She held in her laughter, but was starting to lose her composure.

Markus pretended to take offense. He rubbed his budding chest hairs. "Hey! This is quite the chest of hair, I'll have you know." Just then, his stomach rumbled so loud that her canine ears perked up and she sort of smirked at him. He held his stomach, and with a little blush to his cheeks, said, "I guess it's time for food. What do the Rakki eat for breakfast? More chicken?"

"Sort of. Come with me." She grabbed his hand and pulled him out of the door way and into the village.

"Hey! Wait! Let me get my shirt!" He struggled against the eager way she was tugging him down the street by his hand. When she finally did, he carefully removed her hand from his, ran back, grabbed his shirt, then hurried to follow her. He nearly stumbled into three people while trying to run and put his shirt on at the same time.

Crystal brought Markus to her home, where Treb was fixing a traditional Rakki breakfast. Markus was a little embarrassed to have been brought into their home so suddenly. The way Treb was half dressed, and the fact that Kiin was still getting herself ready for the day, only made Markus even more self-conscious about being there. But, on the other hand, the food smelled really good, and he was starving. Treb was wearing only pants, which showed off his rather impressively muscular physique. After getting a good look at Treb, Markus felt a little less manly, having shown Crystal his not-so-muscular physique.

Crystal directed Markus sit at a large round wooden table, with a circular bench around it that seemed to have been carved out of a single piece of wood. On the table were plates of cooked hen eggs, a pot of soup, and some fresh biscuits Treb had just pulled out of the oven.

Upon seeing the unexpected guest, Treb looked at Crystal with a knowing expression. "I wondered why you asked for a big breakfast this morning. You could've warned us you were expecting to bring him over."

Markus gulped and smiled at him. "I'm glad to be invited. I don't wish to be any trouble, though."

"Oh, you're no trouble. I made enough food for several guests. Crystal must think the Humankind eat a lot of food." He set a bowl on the table with a pile of berries in it. His attitude was downright surly, with a hint of sarcasm in every word.

Crystal gave Treb a frown, then turned to Markus. "This is a complete Rakki breakfast. Do you approve?"

Markus smiled, knowing how much she wanted to impress him.

So, he looked around and nodded. "Yes. It all looks very tasty. The Humankind eat a lot of the same stuff: cooked eggs, biscuits, and fruit. The soup is a little different. We don't often eat soup for breakfast."

Treb set an empty bowl in front of Markus. "That's probably the most common breakfast item on our table. This is a soup made of the leftovers from dinner the night before. Chicken, vegetables, spices, sometimes potatoes, sometimes breads—whatever we have." He set a bowl in front of Crystal, and then set another bowl on the table, right between the other two bowls.

Markus frowned at the bowl placed between his and Crystal's. There wasn't room for another person to sit between them. Besides, the table had more than enough room for several more people, but he said nothing.

Treb plopped a ladle into the soup pot and went to get some cloth napkins and spoons from the counter. "Go ahead and serve yourself."

Markus picked up his spoon and looked at the pot of soup. "Do you mind if I taste it first?"

Crystal was so eager for him to try it, she didn't even say anything; she simply nodded.

He dipped his spoon in and scooped up a single piece of chicken, along with a bit of the heavy broth. First, he blew across it to cool it, then he carefully put it in his mouth. The first flavor was the bright herbs and spices of the chicken. It was good. Then it hit him.

The spice grew and grew. It felt like it was burning a hole through his tongue. His forehead began to sweat, and there were tears forming in his eyes. The burning started on his tongue and then moved to every soft part of his mouth. In fact, his teeth might just have melted. His very first instinct was to spew, but he happened to glance up and see the earnest look on Crystal's face as she waited with a big smile, knowing he would love this soup as much as she did. He didn't want to offend her, and he really thought she was cute, so he didn't want to screw anything up by insulting their food.

Against every ounce of common sense and the fear in his stomach, he swallowed. The whole way down, he felt the spice trying to eat holes in his body. He wasn't sure if he would survive it. Finally, it was down, and the burning was barely beginning to subside. Calmly, and with the appearance of simply having another drink, he picked up his water glass and drank. It was supposed to be a sip, but he downed the whole glass in one single gulp.

"Do you like it? Isn't it wonderful? Treb makes the best soups." Crystal was happy that Markus had gotten to try one of the best foods in all of Gallenor.

Being a teenage boy, he couldn't tell a pretty girl he didn't like her food, especially when that pretty girl showed any interest in him. So, he managed a smile, used his napkin to wipe the sweat from his brow and the tears in his eyes, and nodded. "Oh, it's certainly . . . good." He had done himself in. How was he supposed to eat without having a bowl of that soup? He was doomed.

Markus, always the gentleman, reached over and took Crystal's bowl and filled it first from the pot in the middle of the table. Just as he was about to hand it to her, there came Treb with the napkins. He reached over and sat them down on the table, which blocked Markus from handing her the bowl. Then, the big, beefy Rakki squeezed himself in between Markus and Crystal. He literally pushed Markus down the bench by a good two feet. The whole time, Markus held the bowl, waiting to finish his gallant gesture.

"Oh, I'll get that." Treb picked up Markus' empty bowl, filled it, and then sat it down in front of Crystal.

Markus was defeated and finally sat the bowl down in front of himself. Crystal was rolling her eyes at Treb, nearly snarling at the same time.

"Treb?" Kiin came into the room and called her husband over to her.

"Yes, dear?" He craned his head around, not budging an inch from where he was sitting.

Kiin quietly, but sternly, gestured for him to come over to her.

He reluctantly got up and obeyed. Kiin was already dressed in full armor and glaring at him. When he got to her side, she whispered, "What are you doing? You were practically sitting on them."

"She brought him over and . . . well, he's a boy."

"Yeah, I noticed. The problem?" Kiin knew perfectly well what the problem was, but she wanted to hear it from him.

"He's a teenage boy. And . . . well . . . you should've seen the way he was drooling all over her last night."

Kiin patted his chest. "Sweetheart, you're going to have to relax. They hardly know each other. Besides, I think we have other things to worry about."

"Like what?"

She pulled him over to the window near the door and pointed out. "Look, Norl returned only moments ago, and from the looks of the horse he rode in on, he was racing here."

This quickly got his attention. "Why do you suppose he's in such a hurry? Norl wasn't going to return for another two weeks."

"Something must have happened." Kiin was extremely concerned. The ride from Thendor usually took two full days, and the horse looked, the journey had been completed in just one night. "I don't like it. We should head to the court and find out what's going on."

"Do you think something bad has happened?"

Kiin picked up her bow and slung it around to her back. "I don't know, but I doubt he raced home to bring us a basic court report from Thendor."

Treb looked back at the two kids sitting down to eat. "We should wait until breakfast is over."

"Honey, she's sixteen and has proven herself trustworthy. I'm sure we can leave them here to take care of themselves."

Treb growled a little. "He is also sixteen—at least, he looks about that age—and I don't trust boys around our little girl."

"She isn't a little girl anymore. Besides, Grandmother is upstairs; she'll keep an eye on them. We really do need to go and find out what is going on." Kiin was more logical than Treb when it came to Crystal. Treb had always been the overprotective father, ever since Crystal had become their daughter four years ago.

Treb let out a huff and then nodded. "Fine. I'll go get ready, and I'll wake Grandmother."

"Good. I'll prepare some food for us. Hurry up." Kiin patted his bare chest one last time and then walked toward the kitchen.

Markus strolled through the village with Crystal. He did his best not to pant again, but the sweat across his brow only gave away his discomfort.

Crystal frowned as she observed him wipe his forehead again. "Are you well? Do you have a fever?"

"I'm fine. I'm just getting over the soup. I don't think I've ever eaten anything that spicy before."

She giggled at him. "We always eat soup for breakfast, and it's the spiciest food of the day. Wakes you up."

"Sure does. Though, I suppose my stomach wasn't quite prepared for that level of . . . waking up." He breathed heavy for a moment and gathered himself. "So, who was that kind old lady that helped clean up the kitchen?"

"That's my grandmother, Korini. Well, she is Treb's mother, so she isn't *really* my grandmother."

Markus shrugged. "It's okay. I'm sure she thinks of you as a grandchild. She didn't speak much."

"Grandma is one of the oldest Rakki in the village. She was raised to speak in the old tongue. I can understand her . . . mostly. But, I suppose she didn't want to confuse you. She's a tome of history, though. I could sit and listen to her for hours, talking about the history of the Rakki."

"Speaking of tomes, when are we going to see this library of yours?" Markus tried to hide his impatience, but he was eager to see what the library held.

Crystal gave him a shy grin. "It's just ahead. I've been walking us that direction."

"Oh. Good." He looked ahead and then around. "There aren't any large buildings around here. Where is it?"

"Follow me." She took his hand and pulled him around the wooden walkways and dirt paths of the forest village. Each step seemed to become lower and lower. The paths were leading down to the lowest part of the forest floor.

As they headed lower, Markus saw a large cleared area at the base of some of the trees, where a group of Rakki were practicing with their bows. Some were very young and had teachers all around them, giving direction; others were shooting with the precision that had made the Rakki archers famous.

"Hey, Crystal. Do all Rakki wear the same armor?" Markus noticed even the younger kids had the same style of armor on, which was mostly leather with only a few metal areas for protection.

"Of course. The armor we have is specially made for archers. It moves better with the body so that they can shoot their arrows. Why?"

"I noticed Treb doesn't wear some of it. In fact, he only wears the shoulder pieces on each arm. Has he not earned his armor or something?"

She laughed heartily. "Treb is a master archer—one of the best of the Rakki. The only armor you earn are the shoulder pieces, because they have the symbol of the Arrowguard on them: an extreme honor for any Rakki archer."

"Then where're the leather parts? You know—that cover the chest and back?"

Crystal snickered. "He won't admit this, but when he first courted Kiin, she said that she liked his chest. She liked to look at it. Since then, he's never covered it unless he has to. He'll never say this, but he is a romantic at heart, and his heart is devoted to Kiin."

"That's fine and all, but it must get cold never putting on a shirt."

"Cold? He's got enough fur," Crystal stated very plainly and then laughed.

They walked on and climbed farther and farther down, where the tree trunks grew so thick, it was hard to see around them. The daylight was nearly impossible to find, and the air grew a little cooler with each step.

Crystal stopped them just as they reached an extremely dark area. Markus looked ahead and saw that they were almost beneath the village. He was looking at huge tree roots jutting out from rocks and dirt—the same trees that held the village in place and protected it. In the middle of the intertwining roots was a massive wooden door that was intricately carved with two Rakki warriors, one on each door. The door itself was three times as tall as Markus and very imposing. It did not help that the two carved warriors were snarling at anyone who approached.

"Crystal? Why does this look like a dangerous place?"

"The Rakki were entrusted with many volumes of lore from all over Gallenor. When this facility was first built, only the scholars and leaders were allowed inside. The common people and any outsiders were not welcomed. These warriors on the doors were a message: *Enter at your own risk*." She started pulling on his hand again to head for the doors.

He stopped her. "Are you absolutely sure I'm allowed?"

"Of course. Three generations ago, the library was opened to the world. The only rules you'll need to follow are to not take anything out without permission of the leader of the Rakki . . . And, of course, to not destroy anything."

He cleared his throat, and the little cautious voice in his head began to tell him all the good reasons he could use to back out. But, the prospect of seeing some old spell books, and even a map to where he was headed, was more exciting than his fear. So, he let her tugs finally bring him to the door.

Crystal softly knocked on a special spot on one of the doors. Markus was sure no one could have heard the knock and was about to step up and bang on the wooden door himself. But suddenly, one of the doors opened, and an old Rakki woman stood there, a permanent sour expression on her canine face.

"I wish to bring a friend in to study," Crystal stated.

The old woman glared at Markus for a moment and then nodded to them. Without a single word uttered, she turned and walked away. Crystal pulled Markus inside, her enthusiasm growing with each moment.

Markus came in and was astounded with what he saw. The library was truly built into the trees, with roots growing down everywhere. Huge shelves were built into and around these roots, appearing as though they had grown right out of the tree. On one side, shelves were filled to the brim with books of all descriptions, some bound in leather, others bound in wood. A whole section of shelves were devoted to scrolls from every era of known history. A few texts were just a bit of rolled up paper, while others were massive and held together by large wooden spindles. There was also a collection of special, magical crystals that stored information through unique spells and various other methods of information keeping. There were scribed hides, etched stone, carved bone, and even a few phials of information keeping potions.

"Crystal, this place . . . it's . . . amazing!" Markus was breathless at the sight of all this accumulated knowledge.

Crystal giggled at him. "I told you it was impressive."

He let go of her hand and looked up at the mass of roots growing across the ceiling. "Is the entire Rakki village built over the library?"

"Yes. The village's first purpose was as guardian of this library. It still is an important facet of our lives, but not our only mission any longer. To this day, all Rakki are taught that keeping this place safe and adding to it is our responsibility."

Markus ran over to a shelf and picked up a huge blue crystal with hundreds of ancient Bilmlec letters floating around on the inside. "Is this a memory crystal?" Before she had a chance to answer him, he put it down and grabbed a large black mirror on the same shelf. "It can't be! A mirror of scribing! Is it filled? Whose memories are kept inside?" Again, he ran off before hearing an answer. He snatched another crystal, this one red and glowing. "I heard that the old firebirds crafted these to hold spell knowledge. Is that true?"

Crystal finally broke his frenetic, excited questioning. "Markus! Markus! Calm down, slow down."

Markus realized he was hardly even breathing. Swaying a little, he caught his breath and forced himself to settle down. He calmly set the crystal back on the shelf. "I'm sorry. This is like a dream come true."

"You know so much already. Did your home village have a good library?" Crystal was truly amazed at his knowledge of information keeping.

Markus knew most of it through his strange dreams, but he wasn't quite willing to tell her so just yet. "I, uh, have heard about such items. Just haven't ever seen any." He touched a phial of lore keeping potion and smiled. It was like stepping into one of his nicer dreams about magic. He wanted dearly to bring stuff of this kind out into reality when he woke so he could use them in the real world. Until now, he had wondered if it truly existed; it was *awesome* to behold.

Crystal pointed off toward another part of the library. "Let's go find a table where we can sit down so you don't explode. I'll bring you some of the texts I used to start learning about magic, and you can read them there. We have all day. If you want, I'm sure there's much you can learn in that time."

"Lead the way." He would let her take control of the day, because she knew this place.

Once he sat down, he waited for her to bring his first books. A part of him wanted to stay for a month and study, but another part knew he had a mission to complete. This was an opportunity for him, but it was also a temptation, so he needed to stay focused.

In another part of the village, the large doors to the Rakki courtroom opened, and a single person walked in. It was an old Rakki who came with little fanfare, but all the same, everyone bowed as he passed. Lord Kellus was the leader of the Rakki. He was revered for his wisdom, judgment, patience, and gentleness. Hardly anything happened within the village of which he was unaware. His fur was tinged with grey, his face was drawn a little from age, but otherwise, he was a strong man with a commanding presence.

Kellus walked past the gathered people and nodded with a smile to his most trusted adviser, Lord Norl. Turning around, Kellus addressed the two people who had asked to be informed about what happened to bring Norl back so early from court. "Master Treb and Lady Kiin, I have heard troubling news today. Lord Norl has returned from Thendor with a revelation suggesting the King may be plotting against the kingdom."

Treb stated what he had thought for four years. "That seemed apparent when he ordered all wizards imprisoned for no good reason."

Kellus continued. "What is even worse is that the King is about to send his scouts once again into our lands, searching for more wizards to imprison."

Kiin gasped, "Crystal!" then held her mouth, for fear of having just given away a closely guarded secret.

Kellus smiled and asked, "What is that, Kiin?"

Kiin cleared her throat and gulped. "It seems the daughter of the wizards Shio and Fiona is also a wizard. She works in our medical ward as a healer, like her mother."

Kellus continued to smile. "I know."

Treb looked up at his lord with astonishment. "But, sir, I thought if any wizards were discovered, they were to be sent to the Pale Labyrinth?"

"There are a great many things the King has ordered that have worried me over the past four years. When I learned this little girl had magical abilities, I became concerned for her, just as you are. She does not deserve to be imprisoned for her natural talents, and her parents need to be set free. Our people, the people I protect and rule, deserve the freedoms allotted any living being in Gallenor. The rules set by King Anthony are unfair. It is time we do something about these rules."

Treb was surprised and a little more than curious. "Are we going to go against the King? We're not strong enough to fight the entire Royal Army."

"No. I do not propose such a disastrous plan. But, it is time we find our own answers. The King is seeking something, and we must find it first so he does not use it against anyone." Kellus motioned for Norl to speak.

Norl stepped over and looked at the two best warriors of the Rakki. "The King is seeking the last Dragonwand, rumored to be hidden in the kingdom somewhere. He means to use it to destroy the evil dragon statue, or at least this is what he's led us to believe for these last four years. But, I overheard him speaking with his personal wizard, and his plans are much darker than I had ever anticipated."

Treb had never known Norl to look so disturbed about anything. He was such a calm and collected man that this really bothered Treb. "Lord Norl, what are his plans that are so dark?"

Norl took a moment to get himself together before speaking. After a pause, he looked at Treb with quivering eyes. "Hallond means to kill every wizard trapped in the Pale Labyrinth and use their collected magical strength to cast some sort of immortality spell over the King and himself."

Kiin gasped and held her hand to her mouth, so shocked, she was not able to say anything.

Treb was snarling and even growling. "How dare they! They have no right! We must do something to stop this!" His words echoed throughout the hall.

Kellus slowly nodded in agreement, but he maintained his collected demeanor. "I concur. He cannot obtain the Dragonwand before we have had a chance to find it. You see, we must utilize our vast library to find any information about . . ."

"Did you say Dragonwand?" Kiin interrupted Kellus.

The Rakki leader stopped and nodded. "Yes. Have you heard anything of this?"

Kiin looked at her husband, and he nodded at her to say what they knew. "Uh, Lord Kellus, there's a young Humankind we found near our village yesterday. He spoke to our daughter about a quest he has been sent on to find something called a Dragonwand. I'm not sure if it's the same wand you speak of, though."

Norl was shocked. He nodded quickly and said, "There's only one Dragonwand. The King's men have been searching for it for over four years now, without any luck."

Kellus furrowed his brow and stuck one eyebrow up. "Is this boy still here?"

Treb bowed his head as he answered. "Yes. He and our daughter have gotten to know one another, and she's with him as we speak."

Kellus waved a hand to one of his guards. "Bring him to me."

Kiin stopped him, interrupting him yet again. "Uh, if I may, I'll go and fetch them. "

Kellus waved one more time at the guard to stop him. "Fine, bring them before me."

Kiin and Treb bowed out and left the wooden palace of the Rakki. Once the door was closed, Treb gave Kiin a rather quizzical look. "Why did you volunteer for this? I'm sure the guard would be fine to go get him."

Kiin rolled her eyes at him. "Honey, Crystal has taken a rather quick liking to this boy, and I dare say he likes her too. If guards show up and take him away from her, it might be a little hard on her. I would not want to bring back bad memories over this."

"I . . . I didn't think of it that way. Now, where are they?"

CHAPTER 6: THE WIZARD CODEX

MORA, the librarian, sat at her desk, looking over a chart showing all the shelves in one particular place. It was about time to add another shelf to house the incoming books, because they were running out of room in that department. She drew on the paper and then erased it quickly; mapping out a library wasn't easy, and it was all on her to take care of this right now. *Oh, the trials of being the Head Librarian of the largest known library in the world.*

At that very moment, a huge bird made of fire flew through the library and screamed with a shrill, high pitch. Mora hit the ground, covered her head with her hands, tucked her tail between her legs, and screamed in pure fear. After a few moments of waiting to be incinerated, she realized nothing had happened. Cautiously looking up, Mora realized that nothing was there. No bird, no fire, not even any singe marks on anything. Suddenly, there were thousands of pops and booms coming from another part of the library, which accompanied multicolored flashes of light in the same vicinity.

Mora grabbed a paddle she used to straighten books and marched away from her desk and around several shelves. About half a mile away from her desk, she found Markus and Crystal sitting at a long wooden table. The table was covered with books and scrolls of all kinds, some huge, others small. Markus had his wand out and was producing a spectacular spray of fireworks from the end. In his other hand was a book on illusionary magics.

With a sharp slap of the paddle against the table, Mora got their attention. Markus instantly lost focus and the fireworks stopped. Both kids looked up, seeing the very angry librarian's face as she stood snarling, showing a few sharp canine teeth.

"In this library, we do not cause such disturbances," she reprimanded. "If you do not refrain from using that wand of yours, I'll be forced to ask you to leave!"

Crystal, who was standing, gulped and tucked her tail. "Uh . . . sorry."

Markus grinned nervously. "I won't do it anymore. I promise."

"Good." Mora stopped snarling and left them to their books.

Once Markus and Crystal saw the last of the librarian's tail, they both started laughing.

Crystal sat down next to Markus and wiped her eyes. "I've never seen her so angry before."

He closed the spell book he had been reading. "I'm sorry if I got you in any trouble." The apology came out through his chuckling.

"It's all right. It was kind of funny." She finished chuckling. "I'm astonished. You can cast spells with ease and power. How is this possible?"

Markus looked at his wand. "I think it's partly due to this powerful wand, and partly an innate knowledge."

"Innate knowledge?"

Markus decided it would be okay to tell her about his dreams, at least in a small amount. "I've grown up with dreams about magic. Not every night, but often. I don't know how or where they come from, but I've this sense about magic. It always seemed to come naturally to me. I think it is why Tolen chose me for this mission."

Crystal was awed. "Do you even need the spell books?"

"Of course." Markus sat up straighter and looked at all the books they had already flipped through. "My knowledge is rough and undefined. I can do some things, but a great deal more is far beyond my understanding. It's kinda like when you watch your mom cooking something, but when you try, it just doesn't come out the same way."

"You need instruction from someone, or in this case, something with experience," Crystal finished the thought.

"Yes, exactly. I have an understanding how the spell will look and a little about casting it, but the fine details, the bits and pieces that make it come out right, aren't there. Just looking through this library's collection of magical items and tomes, I can finally understand some of the magic I've seen in my dreams for all these years. I have to remember that firebird spell. I could put a little fear into Tolk when I get back." There was devilishness in his tone.

"Tolk? A friend of yours?"

"Hardly," Markus scoffed. "He's another farmer who thought I was a fool for wanting to pursue my magical ambitions. He's a rather nasty person."

"Did you have many friends where you're from?" Crystal asked as she began to gather up some of the books they had already looked through.

Markus opened a manual on healing magics and flipped through it. "Not really. Most of the other kids my age were farmers, just like their parents. Oh, when we were little, we all played and had fun. But as we grew up, I became the oddball, the outcast. They didn't understand magic and feared me. I guess I was a bit of a showoff with my talents—what little I could do. I wish I'd known more people like you . . . people not afraid of me."

"I'm glad you are here, too. I don't have a lot in common with other kids around here. They aren't mean to me or anything like that; they just like doing other things. Of course, if I had a great wand like yours, I might be more popular."

Markus held up the wand in his hand and looked it over. "It's a really nice thing to have. Though, I'm still not sure if I can use it to its fullest potential. Tolen probably expected I knew more of what I was doing."

"You seem to know a lot more than you give yourself credit. You hardly had to try to cast any of those spells."

"It's a powerful wand, and illusionary magic isn't really that hard. Healing magic . . . now, that's hard. I'd be scared to death to use it, for fear my first try at healing someone would set them on fire." He cringed at the idea.

Crystal shook her head. "Healing magic isn't that hard. I do it all the time."

"Don't I know it. Your healing magic saved me from a broken arm in a sling." He flashed her a boyish grin.

She looked at him and smiled right back. "It was just a broken bone. Simple magic."

He was about to say something but got lost in her eyes for a moment. The torchlight in the library was shining in her crystal blue eyes, and he was transfixed. When he had first met her, he couldn't get past the tail and fur. It was a shocking idea for him to see a girl covered in so much hair. Yet now, all he could do was look at her eyes and marvel at how beautiful they were.

"Markus?" Crystal saw the way he was looking at her and slunk down in embarrassment.

He coughed and shook off the moment. "I . . . uh . . . I was just looking at . . . uh . . . hey, didn't you say you had a map of the old places in Gallenor?"

She bit her lower lip and nodded. "Yeah, there's a book with information about the old forts and temples of Gallenor. It should have a map in it. I know where it is. I will . . . be . . ." She trailed off when she heard a familiar voice talking to Mora at the desk across the library.

Markus, without a Rakki's ears, did not know what was taking her attention away. "Crystal?"

She stood up. "I hear my father."

Just then, Treb, Kiin, and Mora came around a shelf, all looking at Markus.

Markus smiled, but was scared to death. "Uh, hi. What is it?"

Treb looked at his daughter, then at Markus. "Come with us. Lord Kellus wishes to see you."

"Lord Kellus?" Markus squeaked out, a terrible fear bubbling up in his belly.

Crystal quietly answered, "Kellus is our leader."

Markus gulped and started explaining himself. "It was just an illusionary spell. I didn't set anything on fire. I didn't mean to scare her to death. It was just an . . . accident."

"What are you talking about?" Kiin asked in bewilderment.

Markus' eyes darted to the librarian and then back to the others. "Aren't I in trouble?"

"No, Lord Kellus just wishes to meet you," Treb answered.

Crystal set down a book she was holding. "Me, too?"

"No," Kiin gently answered, and saw a desire in her daughter's eyes. "If you want, you can come, too."

Markus and Crystal joined Treb and Kiin as they all left the library together. Markus was as nervous as he could be, but glad he was not going alone.

Crystal was more than curious, but asked no questions yet.

Markus did his best to act grown up. He was turning sixteen in two days, and he needed to act it. Though, on the inside, he was shaking so hard, his stomach was quivering.

The giant wooden doors to the Grand Hall were opened, and two guards with Treb, Kiin, Crystal, and Markus all walked down the long path toward the throne. The Grand Hall was impressive. Not quite as much as the library beneath the city, but it was certainly amazing to see. Everything inside was carved from wood: the tables, chairs, columns . . . even the large fire pit itself, in the center of the room, was made of wood. The fire pit had a roaring fire in the middle of rocks placed just so to keep the whole hall from going up in a blaze.

Dozens of Rakki stood around, watching people enter the room. Of course, their eyes were all on Markus, for it had been a long time since a Humankind that was not a member of the Royal Guards had set foot in here. Most of the people in the Grand Hall were in armor, not unlike Treb's or Kiin's. They were the warriors of the Rakki, commanders and their lieutenants.

Markus was stopped by Treb's strong hand as they got to the throne. Then, with a firm press, Treb forced Markus to kneel as they all came down to one knee. It was an honor to be summoned by Kellus, but right then, Markus felt like he was about to face punishment for . . . something.

"So, you are the young wizard who has befriended our little Crystal," Kellus spoke with a collected, wise voice.

Markus looked up, cleared his throat, and then tried to speak. His mouth was dry, and his voice was suddenly gone.

Treb patted him on the back. "This is Markus, the Humankind who saved Kiin outside the village with an impressive spell."

Kellus smiled and stuck up one furry eyebrow. "Is this true? Do you control magic with such precision to combat an imp?"

Markus cleared his throat again and then nodded. "Ye . . . yes, sir. I, uh, used magic. I have this wand, and well, I used it to stop that imp thing."

"Imps are quite the problem for our people in these trees. They infest the Blue Forest and cause trouble wherever they are found. Recently, they have been getting worse. A sign of darker times coming." Kellus changed the flow of discussion with one question. "Tell me, young Markus, do you seek the Dragonwand?"

This got Markus' attention. He knew Tolen had sent him to find that particular item, but he wasn't sure about anyone else looking for it. What could they possibly want with it? "I am. Why?"

"Markus," Treb harshly whispered at the boy, for the question was not asked with the respect Markus should have given for such an honored elder.

"It is all right, Master Treb. He has the right to ask," Kellus interceded for Markus, then turned his attention back to the boy. "We have heard troubling words from our King about that wand. It seems he seeks it too, and does so for villainous desires. Are you seeking it to present to him or to keep it from him?" Kellus asked as calmly as he might ask for a glass of water.

Markus was curious. Tolen had not given him much information. "I was asked to find it so I might present it to a statue outside of Thendor. I guess that means I'll keep it away from the King. Is he a bad person?"

Kellus spoke like a sage. "Good or bad is such an uncertain idea. The King's plans are good—in his mind. But his means will result in bad things happening. For us, his actions are bad."

"What do you want of me?"

"I would like to know if you have the wand or know where it is. For it is paramount we locate it and keep it safe."

Markus shook his head. "I don't have it, and I'm not entirely certain where to find it. I was sent on a quest for it, but received very little information to guide me."

Kellus rubbed his furry chin. "It seems the problem I face and your quest have crossed paths. The King seized and imprisoned a number of my people four years ago. He lied to us, saying they would be freed once the wand was found and the kingdom was again safe. Now, we know he means to destroy all wizards and to craft a most devious magic with the help of his head wizard. Finding the wand will not only prevent him from finishing this spell, but could help free my people and many others."

Crystal gasped, and then made an uncontrollable whimper as she started to panic. Her parents could be killed by this King. Her worst nightmares were coming true.

Markus carefully put a hand on hers, since she was kneeling

beside him. Then he whispered, "I won't let that happen." He meant this for her ears only, but he misjudged the ears of the Rakki around him.

Kellus was highly intrigued by this comment. An almost sneaky smile crossed his face. "I see you do mean to stop him. I am glad to hear that."

Markus eagerly smiled and stood up. "Then you want my help?"

Kellus did not return the eagerness, and only a raised eyebrow and glance of scrutiny. "It seems you need our help. We have information you could use to find the wand. But . . ." He paused and continued to look over Markus.

Markus gulped and asked, "What?"

"I am not sure if I can trust you." He didn't say so for Markus as much as for someone else in the room.

All four people stayed silent before the Lord of the Rakki. Treb looked at his wife, and both shrugged, not understanding what Kellus wanted to hear.

Markus felt every eye on him. He started to sweat and shifted from foot to foot. Then he asked, "How may I prove myself to you?"

Kellus shook his head. "I cannot say. I know none of your triumphs or actions, other than one spell that saved Lady Kiin. If only I had spent time with you."

Crystal cleared her throat and stood up from her kneeling position. She was standing right next to Markus. "Sir, if I might speak, please." She was so scared, her tail was down between her legs, and she was visibly shaking. Both Treb and Kiin were shocked she even spoke at all.

Kellus tipped his head to her. "What would you say, child?"

She looked at Markus and then at her lord. "I've spent time with him. It's only been an evening and today, but I've found a person who is kind and funny. He hasn't done anything to harm me or show greed in any fashion, save perhaps a healthy taste for knowledge. He showed me some magic I had always wished to see, though it did startle Mora in the library. And when Mora came to ask him to stop, he was obedient."

Kellus held his hand out to Markus. "So, Crystal, you vouch for this Humankind?"

She nodded her head, her tail still tucked and her hands shaking. "Yes."

Markus looked at her with a friendly, happy smile. He had no idea she would say such things about him. "Thanks."

Kellus stood up from his throne and bowed his head to Markus. "Then, you have my blessing for your quest."

Treb muttered to Kiin, "His blessing because a sixteen-year-old girl likes this boy?"

Kellus gave Treb a knowing grin. "Master Treb, you may view your little girl as a mere sixteen-year-old child, but I have come to understand her scrutiny. She would not so quickly befriend someone, and I dare say she would need a good reason to show the courage to speak up in here when she did. This Markus must be a special boy to encourage that in this young lady."

Markus bowed to Kellus. "Thank you, sir."

Treb had the most embarrassed look on his face for being corrected in front of everyone. He had thought only his wife would hear his words.

Just then, Norl hurried in from another part of the Grand Hall. In his arms, he carried a large item wrapped in cloth. "I found it! I found it!"

Kellus looked back to see his first courtier come running. "And not a moment too soon." He stepped down from his throne to speak with Norl, away from the others.

Treb and Kiin both stood up from their kneeling and approached Markus and Crystal. Treb had a worried look on his canine features, while Kiin was proud of her girl. No one spoke yet, for they knew Kellus was not finished.

"Markus, step forward." Kellus stood at the side of his throne with a large, leather-bound book in his hands.

Markus straightened his shoulders and came over to the Rakki lord. "Yes, sir?"

Kellus held out the book. "This is for you."

Markus wasn't sure what to do or say as he took the book. The leather had words scribed into it, but he could not read them. He slowly opened the book, finding the pages filled to the brim with the same words, written in a language he could not read. "What is it?"

Norl answered, "That is the Wizard Codex. It was put together by an ancient wizard, just after the War."

Markus was amazed at the idea of holding a book that could possibly be over a thousand years old. "Wow . . . what do I do with it?"

Kellus walked Markus back to the front of the throne with the others. "This was created as a means for future generations to harness the knowledge of the ancients. The wizard who crafted this gave it to the first Rakki lord, instructing him to keep it safe until a time came when the kingdom was threatened by dark magics. The Codex holds the secrets of the Dragon Citadel, and even some spells that have long been lost to the wizards of Gallenor. With this, you should be able to complete your quest."

Markus looked at the book again. Opening it up, he tried to

decipher the words. "I . . . I'm sorry, but the wizard who sent me on this journey didn't take the time to teach me ancient wizard tongue. I can't read this."

"I know," Kellus stated very frankly. "No one can. The words are written with a magic spell. The wizard who gave this to us said only ancient knowledge can unlock ancient knowledge."

Markus rolled his eyes and scoffed. "What does that mean?"

Treb slapped Markus in the arm. "Show more respect."

Kellus was chortling. "It's okay, Master Treb. He is right to be frustrated." He returned his attention to the young man. "Markus, no one has ever understood what that statement means. I am sure you will discover the meaning when the time is right. Fortunately, there is more to this than coded words." He approached Markus and turned the pages all the way to the back. The very last page and cover were connected. The long page wasn't simply more words. It was a map. "The wizard gave you this much information. See there." He pointed to a small indicator over the mountains in the north. "That directs you to the Barren Mountains. This is the only known map that reveals any sort of location involving the Dragon Citadel. We have kept this secret for many generations, waiting for the day when an honest man came seeking it."

Treb, unaware of this legendary book and map, asked, "Why haven't you given this to the King? He has said many times that they're seeking the Citadel."

Kellus smiled at his warrior. "The King showed incredible foolishness by taking so many of our people. I felt he had not proven himself worthy of seeing this. After nearly fifty generations of waiting, we had to be certain of the person who was to be given this Codex."

Treb scoffed and shook his head in disbelief. "And you choose a boy, a Humankind boy? What kind of logic is that?"

Kellus simply smiled, while Kiin just about swallowed her teeth at her husband's outburst. "Master Treb, if you see reason to not trust this boy, please volunteer to go with him."

"Huh?" Treb, Kiin, and Markus all responded in unison.

Kellus nodded to them. "If you are so worried about his intentions and worthiness of such a gift and task, then you should go with him, seeing to it that he completes this task to your specifications. I am sure he would welcome such a talented and noble warrior of the Rakki."

Markus realized he was meant to answer. "Oh . . . uh . . . yeah. Any help would be welcomed."

Treb frowned and looked at his wife. "Kiin?"

Kiin gave it a moment of thought and then honestly answered, "It's the chance of a lifetime to visit the Dragon Citadel and help free our people."

"So . . . you're saying you want to go?" Treb was confused and a bit shocked.

Kiin looked at Crystal. She remembered the week after Crystal's parents were taken from her—how she had cried and cried. The memory alone made Kiin's heart ache. "I've waited too long to give this child back to her own mother and father. It's about time we force the issue and rescue them ourselves. And, as I see it, helping Markus is the only opportunity we have ever had to finally see our friends again. To see Crystal home with her real parents once more."

Treb's mind momentarily ran with a flood of thoughts. There were questions and concerns about every aspect of this journey. He looked at Crystal. She was precious to him . . . a child who relied on him and Kiin for safety and support. They provided her with a home and family, but no one could truly replace her parents. It was time he gave her what she wanted the most in life. So, he set aside all his many questions and thoughts and simply nodded to Kellus. "Yes, I guess this is what I would want, too. I'll go with him."

Kiin took Treb's hand and looked at Kellus. "*We* will go with him."

Kellus smiled at Markus, who had two of the proudest, most skilled warriors of the Rakki standing behind him. "Go then, with my blessing, and bring my people back home."

CHAPTER 7: SEARCHING

HALLOND left the city of Thendor and rode alone far into the countryside where the Desolate Mountains spread out. The mountains were dirty, barren, and considered as the badlands by many. The only prestige the mountains held was in their history. It was across these mountains that the ancient wizards had waged a war over a thousand years ago. Through battles and many terrible spells, the mountains were stripped of any use other than to keep the harsh winter winds of the north from besieging Thendor.

To Hallond, these mountains were home. He had lived and fought here many times during the War. He rode higher and higher into the mountains, cutting through narrow passes at which the horse hesitated. Hallond had a destination in mind and a thin smile on his lips. Once he came to a sheer cliff that provided nothing but a dead end, he knew he was where he wanted to stop. He dismounted his horse and tethered her to a stump of a long-dead tree that had made a futile attempt at growing there. He pulled out his wand and approached a stack of boulders that were much too heavy for any person to lift.

"Vega!" he called out, and a blue glow surrounded the boulders, lifting them up as clouds into the air. Carefully, he stacked them around a newly revealed cave entrance. Once the blue glow was gone, he walked fearlessly onward.

The cave was not carved by time, but by magic. The cavern was huge and constructed with many large crevasses. Hundreds of boxes were scattered around the cave. Each held a person-sized object. As Hallond walked into the cave, torches on the walls instantly ignited and provided light. This illuminated the multitude of objects spread about the room. Mirrors, swords, shields, a few skeletons, crystals, and other various magical items, were all that remained of the dark wizards' relics after the War.

"Who goes there?!" a ghostly voice echoed throughout the cave.

Hallond rolled his eyes. "Must we do this every time?"

"Announce yourself, or be destroyed!" the same voice said, threatening him.

With a bored expression and unexcited voice, he replied, "It is I, Hallond. No one else is with me."

Suddenly, hundreds of ghostly people made of shadowy smoke that shimmered in red hues rose up from the boxes. It was like a great fire had been lit, though the cavern was colder.

A balding male ghost glared at Hallond. "Are you ready for us?!"

"No."

Many of the ghosts began to speak, all angry with him.

He raised his hands to get their attention. "Silence!" The voices slowly stopped, but the anger was still present in their faces. "The plan is still on track. Once we obtain the Dragonwand . . ." The very mention of the word sent a wave of incensed growls and harsh words. Hallond continued despite them, "Once we obtain the Dragonwand, I will have the power I require to complete the spell."

A woman hovering near a box that leaned up against a wall asked, "What of the bodies? Will we have enough?"

Hallond gave off a rather evil smile. "Yes. I have thousands of perfect bodies awaiting you. Each is carrying the wizard gene, so you will be able to seize it without worry."

The first man to speak did not stop glaring at him. "Your own spell will break soon. If you do not complete this mission, you will no longer be able to walk with the living. All our plans, our triumphant return, will be destroyed."

It never ceased to agitate Hallond to listen to someone describe how he could possibly fail. He stepped up to the ghost hovering over his own coffin. "I will succeed. Tolen has died, and no one stands between the Dragonwand and us. All that remains is locating the Dragon Citadel. Once the King's Guards find the wand, all your concerns will be put to rest. Do not worry."

"What of the King?" another man asked. "He suspects nothing?"

Hallond turned and walked around, a wicked smile playing delicately on his lips. "The King is a foolish, greedy human. The mere suggestion that I could make him more powerful only feeds the natural greed they all have. It has blinded him, just as I said it would. He will do anything for me, so long as I keep promising him immortality." Hallond looked into a handheld, gold-lined mirror, sneering at his own face. "And, when I am done with him, I will discard him and take his place as King. I will gain control over Gallenor and herald the new future we were denied those ten centuries ago." He was speaking more to himself than to the ghostly shadows.

The balding ghost looked up. "I sense Tolen's power still at work!"

Hallond's snarl turned to another eye roll. "You sound just like that idiot King. Tolen simply set into motion a plan to stop us. With his death, it will surely fail, and I will win. Do not worry."

"I sense it, too. A wand . . . a wand endowed with ancient magic." The woman by the wall cradled her head with her ghostly hands. The thought of what she sensed in Gallenor right now brought a level of pain.

Hallond turned around and looked at her. "What is this? You must be wrong."

"The eye! Get to the eye!" An old woman pointed to a large ruby on the ground.

Hallond ran over and picked up the ruby, which was as large as a
melon. He peered into it and said, "Tolen." The eye lit up, and began
to search Gallenor for any trace of the ancient wizard Tolen.
Suddenly, a wand appeared, sitting on a table. It was the wand Tolen
had given to Markus. "See, nothing but a relic of that old fool,
nothing to worry—what is this?!" He then saw Markus' hand reach
down and pick up the wand. And every ghost in the cave knew that
any wand enchanted with ancient magic was impossible to hold
unless one was the wand's owner.

"So, Tolen is dead?" the bald man asked sarcastically.

Hallond glared into the crystal. "Show me its user, dammit!" He
couldn't see the person holding the wand. It followed the wand itself,
then turned blurry and stopped showing him anything. "Tolen!"
Hallond dropped the ruby, as he suddenly realized whoever was the
bearer of that wand was being protected by magic from the wizard
Tolen. He couldn't use magic to see the bearer.

A woman called out, "Destroy him!"

Another man yelled, "We are lost!"

The bald ghost held out his hand to silence everyone, and then he
spoke. "Obviously, you underestimated Tolen's foresight. He has
found a way to continue his mission through someone else."

Hallond gathered himself and responded, "Whomever that old fool decided to use will regret helping him. Do not forget: not only do I have every Guard and warrior under the King at my command, but I am still an ancient wizard. We will find them, and we will stop them."

"While continuing the search for the Dragonwand," the woman by the wall stated.

"Yes, of course," Hallond scoffed. "All will still go according to plan. Do not worry, my brothers and sisters. We will not be stopped. The War is not yet over."

"You should send a thousand guards to search each road," the old woman said.

Another called out, "Call a fire demon to scour the lands until the wand bearer is dead."

And another said, "Poison the water of all the villages. That will take care of it."

Hallond turned around and simply walked out. The ghosts had not seen the light of day, or even the ground in front of their own coffins, for a thousand years. They did not know what to do, but he did. Even after stepping out into the daylight, he could still hear them giving him their ideas. With a swift swipe of his hand, the rocks around the cave all tumbled back into place and sealed them into their natural catacomb.

Mounting his horse once more, Hallond rode off out of the mountains. Even though he had an obligation to bring these ancient wizards back to Gallenor, he was pleased with the idea of being their ruler. Once all his plans were complete and he was supreme immortal King of Gallenor, all knees would bow to him—even these old fools.

Markus followed Treb and Kiin out of the village, heading north down a path opposite to the entrance he had come in. Once they were on the road outside of the main forest, Markus looked up to see the blue skies. Though he could see sky above the trees, it felt awfully closed in inside the village. Out here, he felt better.

Kiin had gotten Markus some extra clothes and helped him pack for a walking journey. Treb made sure they had food for the first leg of their trip. They would resupply as they came across markets. Otherwise, when the food ran out, Treb would hunt.

Ever since he had "volunteered," Treb had worn a sour look on his face, as though he were unhappy with everything. Markus wasn't sure if the fearsome warrior was angry at him, or just displeased with having to go along, but he had not braved asking Treb or Kiin about it. Markus was happy to have traveling companions, especially warriors who were very skilled. He wasn't sure how to handle an imp attack if he came across one by himself. He had been lucky last time.

"So, uh, how far are we going to walk today?" Markus asked.

Treb did not look back to answer. "As far as we can get. We're going to have to travel off of the main roads as much as possible, so it'll take a little extra time."

"Off the main roads? Is that safe?"

Kiin shook her head. "Not any less safe than running into a scouting party from Thendor. Wouldn't want them to discover you and your wand and have them cart you off to the Pale Labyrinth."

"Let us worry about what we encounter," Treb stated spitefully. "You need to decipher that book, so we know what to do when we get to the mountains."

Kiin stepped over to him and whispered, "Ease up. He didn't do anything to you."

Treb whispered right back, "We had to leave Crystal behind, by herself. She's left to be worried about yet another set of parents while this boy has filled her mind with hopeful thoughts of seeing her real parents again."

"That's what we're trying to do," Kiin stated clearly.

"Yes, but . . . our little girl has been let down so much, I just cannot stand her having her hopes dashed by an unsuccessful

116

journey." His whispers were harsher than Kiin's, and he was having a hard time keeping Markus from hearing them.

"Give him a chance. Crystal likes him, and he hasn't done anything to hurt anyone. Besides, what makes you think this will be unsuccessful?"

"We're pinning all our hopes on a young Humankind who hardly knows how to use the wand he was given, and doesn't know how to read a book that's all the information we have. And, none of us know what to expect at the Citadel, if we *do* find it."

Kiin smiled at him. "Give him a chance. If you set in your mind failure, then we'll fail. Show a little optimism. Besides, that little boy saved my life, didn't he?"

Treb reluctantly nodded in agreement. "Fine. At least we have him here, and Crystal is back in the village."

"And what do you mean by that?" Kiin knew exactly what he meant, but wanted him to say it.

Treb glanced back at the curious Markus watching them. "At least he won't be flirting with her and giving her . . . ideas."

Kiin laughed at him. "You forget you were just as bad a flirt at his age, and gave a lot of girls some pretty naughty thoughts, including me."

"And, so, I should know exactly what goes through his mind

every time he sees her tail."

Kiin rolled her eyes and stopped walking so close to him. She then spoke with the intention of Markus hearing. "Yes, you do. And I know exactly what she would have done to him if he had touched her wrong. He might have a wand, but she has claws. I remember that night I scratched you so hard that . . ."

Treb's eyebrows lifted and his eyes widened as he shot her a *shut up* glare. "Kiin!"

Markus moved a little closer to them as they walked. "Um, what's the big discussion?"

Kiin smiled at Treb while she answered Markus. "Just talking about tails and claws."

"Oh, Rakki stuff."

Treb nodded while he continued to glare at his wife, praying that she did not finish her last story. "Yeah, Rakki stuff. My lovely wife was reminding me of how dangerous a Rakki girl can be when she receives unwanted advances." His words were meant to inspire a healthy fear.

Markus remained oblivious. "Huh?"

Kiin laughed and took Markus by the shoulder so she might move him next to them, instead of him following behind. "Nothing, dear. We were just reminded that some things are similar between cultures. Girls can be fickle around boys, no matter if they're human or Rakki. Did you have any—" She was about to ask him about his girlfriends back where he was from, but something caught her ears, and she stopped and turned to look behind them. There wasn't any immediate threat, so she did not pull out her bow.

Treb stopped, as did Markus. Both looked back at Kiin.

Treb asked, "What is it?"

She frowned and then waited a moment to listen again. It was gone. "I don't know. I could swear I heard someone or something behind us, but . . . it's gone now."

"Great, imps are tracking us already," Treb grumbled. "Be on your guard."

Markus shifted the large book in his arms to one arm, and prepared himself in case he needed to call his wand. He felt a little more confident, now that he had learned a few new spells, but he was still scared to death of actual combat. "What should we do?"

Treb pointed forward. "We should keep moving. Imps are easily distracted and will often lose interest in whatever they are tracking."

"Especially if they see a shiny object," Kiin added.

All three continued walking down the dirt road. Markus quietly searched his pocket with his free hand and found a small amount of shiny copper coins he had brought with him. He tossed one out, something he would do every hour or so, just to help ward off any imp attacks.

The Grand Hall of the Rakki was back to business as usual, and Kellus resumed looking over paperwork and listening to petitions from the people. Right then, he spoke with one of the High Tree Guards that managed the lookout for the village.

"Kellus!" A guard burst through the doors and came running toward the throne.

Lord Kellus stopped looking over a defense report and waited for the poor young boy to catch his breath. "For goodness' sake. What is it?"

"Royal Guards. They just entered the village. The Captain's at the door of the library, speaking with Mora right now."

Kellus stood up and walked toward the entrance. "Go and summon them to meet with me. I should like to know what they're doing here."

"Yes, at once." The boy bolted off again, leaving the elderly Rakki leader to calmly make his way to the front of the hall.

Captain Morris marched through the town, up to the hall with three of his guards. He did not like being summoned by anyone other than the King, and he certainly did not like being informed of a summons by a mere child. Approaching the hall, he saw the lord of these people waiting on him.

"Lord Kellus. We're here to take any wizards you may have into custody." Morris got right to the point as he stepped up the wooden steps of the hall. He should have bowed in respect, as Kellus technically held a higher rank, but Morris hardly bowed for anyone except the King.

Kellus smiled at him. "You already did, four years ago."

"Yes, and in that four years, your young might have come into their abilities and become wizards. It's important they come with us." Morris was used to giving everyone commands, even the leaders of the different peoples around Gallenor.

With a clever and composed smile, Kellus calmly asked, "Why?"

"Why?! How dare you question royal decrees!"

The old Rakki was not afraid of these men, for he knew full well there were two dozen of the best Rakki archers hiding amongst the trees. If this man decided to dispatch the leader, he would hardly get his sword pulled halfway out before he was punctured multiple times. So, with that same cool, collected tone, he answered. "Yes, I question it. What purpose is there in stealing free people who have done nothing wrong? What purpose is there in taking young people who are just growing up with natural talents?"

Morris stepped up and went face to face with the old Rakki. Morris was a loyal servant, and anyone who questioned the King was not welcomed in his presence. "That is no concern of yours." The truth was that he was not entirely certain as to the meaning behind such orders, but he would never question orders by the King.

Kellus maintained eye contact with Morris. "You may search if you wish. I am sure you will find nothing." There was a certainty in his attitude that was not in the attitudes of the others around him who were all well aware of Crystal's talents.

Morris smiled and cocked his head. "Interesting to hear you say that. One of your own just told me of a girl Dogkind that has researched magic in your library and uses her magic as a healer."

Kellus did not break his composure, though he made a mental note of speaking with Mora as soon as these people left. "That is an interesting story. Should we find out then?" He held out his hand toward the medical house.

Morris signaled for his men to follow him, and he marched off toward the hospital where Crystal was sure to be working right now. With Markus, Treb, and Kiin gone, there was not much for her to do but work and wait. Morris had already visited the library and not found her, so it was just a matter of time before he entered the infirmary.

The doctors and nurses that manned the infirmary were hard at work, helping the Rakki needing medical attention. They were certainly not prepared for a brute slamming open their door and coming right at them with a stone held out in his palm.

Morris marched into the infirmary while he held out a black stone that had been enchanted by Hallond. This stone, when held next to a wizard, changed from solid black to glowing red. No wizard could avoid the stone, or hope to hide their power from its scrutiny. First, Morris held the stone next to the head doctor, then went down the line to each nurse. Everyone in the ward was nervously glancing back at the room where Crystal normally worked.

"They're clear," Morris declared.

The doctor straightened his glasses and cleared his throat. "Then, you may go, unless you require any medical attention."

Morris glared at him. He had been through this enough times to know people would say or do anything to get it over with. It was not their place to decide when the inspection was over. He pushed past them and shoved aside the curtain to Crystal's room.

Everyone watched while Morris held up his stone. All that they could see was his back as he worked. After a terrifying few moments, he went on, leaving the man who was in the bed. No one else was in the room. This surprised everyone, save Kellus, who was standing at the door.

Morris put the stone away and walked up to Kellus. "Where are they?"

Kellus smiled at Morris and shrugged. "I do not know of whom you speak. Perhaps you were misinformed."

Morris practically pushed the elder Rakki down as he left the infirmary. His lieutenant stated, "We need to be moving if we're to reach Riverton by nightfall."

Kellus, containing his contempt for this man, nodded to them. "Yes, please be on your way. Your presence is unsettling to my people."

Morris turned to the leader of the Rakki and nearly snarled. "We will come and go as we please."

"I, Lord Kellus of the Rakki, ask that you leave at once. If any wizards are in our trees, we will dutifully send them to the Pale Labyrinth. This is not a request now; it is an order."

"Why, you—" Morris lifted his hand, ready to strike the old man hard enough to send him across the ground.

Everyone gasped, and yet, Kellus didn't even flinch. Just as Morris was going to brutalize the Rakki Lord, an arrow came out of nowhere and struck the wall right next to him, its shaft skimming the side of his arm to show how dangerously close he was to death if he proceeded. This stopped him mid-motion, and he had a look of actual fear in his wide eyes that were glued on the arrow protruding from the wall.

Kellus stopped looking pleasant and got right in Morris' face. "You may have the authority of the King behind you, but as is written into the Constitutional Concordat signed by all the races, including yours, I still have authority in these lands, and you will recognize that or be subject to my punishment. Captain Morris, unless you have substantial reason to violate the rights of my people any further, you will take your men and leave."

Morris did not like the laws being thrown into his face. He could have done something about the threat on his life, but he knew when it was time to back down—for now. With a single finger pointed at Kellus' face, he made his final point. "This isn't over, old man. You dogs will learn your place in time. For now, I have a job to do and little time to do it. Men, mount up and move out." After he gave this order, he practically stomped away with his soldiers.

The head nurse came out, still shaken by the experience. "Lord Kellus, where's Crystal? Have you hidden her?"

Kellus' eyes were fixed on watching the soldiers leave his village. He answered softly, "No, she is exactly where she should be. Do not worry."

CHAPTER 8: CAMPING UNDER THE STARS

A full day passed as the trio traveled toward the north. Treb, Kiin, and Markus left the worn path and made their way into the trees of a small forest at the base of the foothills. It was Treb's idea to hide in the trees so they would be less noticeable by anything, scout or imp. And, as a Rakki, he simply felt more comfortable in the forest.

Treb had gone to hunt dinner while Kiin and Markus set up camp for the night. Markus gathered wood and kindling, and Kiin prepared some logs to sit on and rolled out the sleeping blankets. Treb and Kiin were experienced hunters trained in tracking down imps and other undesirable creatures that threatened the lands of the Rakki. So, to them, this was just another day of sleeping under the stars and watching their backs for unwanted attacks. Markus wasn't as used to this. He did have some experience in sleeping on the ground by now, but it was still not the most comfortable life for him.

Markus sat on a log and watched Kiin arrange the wood and stones for the fire she hoped would soon be burning. The entire time, he pondered Treb's attitude. He finally gathered the nerve to ask, "So, uh, Kiin, why is Treb so . . . not nice around me?"

Kiin stopped fidgeting with the kindling and firewood and looked at Markus. "Treb is a little overprotective of Crystal. When he saw her connecting with you, his fatherly instincts sort of overshadowed his thoughts, and he took a disliking to you."

"But, I didn't do anything wrong."

"You're a boy; that's wrong enough." She saw the curiosity written all over his face. "Listen, Treb isn't a mean person, and he'll get over this soon enough. You didn't do anything wrong, and he'll see that, some day."

"Crystal's old enough to have boyfriends. I would hate to think every time a boy asks her out, they're going to get the sour attitude of Treb," Markus said.

Kiin let out a sigh and brushed her hands off. She sat next to Markus and gave him a gentle smile. "Treb wants to be a father. It has been his desire since before we married. When Crystal came to us, he got what he had always wanted. We both know she isn't ours, and when her parents return, we will no longer be her parents. But, for now, we have a heartbroken child who needs a protective mother and father."

"Why didn't you two have a child of your own?"

"I've never been able to have a child." Kiin looked down in shame. "The doctors think I'm unable to conceive. I'll never give him a son or daughter of his own. So, you can understand how much it has meant to him to get the opportunity to be a father, even for a short while."

Markus began to understand. "So, when Crystal was smiling and laughing at me, wanting to bring me over and spend time with me, I was taking her away from him."

"In his mind, yes. Also, he's the father of a girl, and as such, he believes all teenage boys are after one thing. And it isn't conversation." Kiin shot him a smirk.

Markus' eyes widened, and he nearly fell off the log. "I . . . I would never!"

Kiin laughed at him. "I know. I also know our little girl isn't so little and can handle a hormonal boy if he *did* try something. But Treb still sees the little girl who came to us the day her parents were taken. He still wants to put his arms around her and protect her from all sadness and harm. And he wants to forget she's done a lot of growing up in the last four years."

"Is that why she didn't come with us?"

"Yes, but I agreed with him on that point. Crystal didn't need to come with us."

Just then, Treb stepped over the other log Kiin had set out and flopped a dead deer on the ground in front of them. "Dinner!" he announced.

Kiin sneered at it. "You could've pulled the arrow out before bringing it here."

Treb rolled his eyes, knelt down, and unceremoniously ripped the arrow out of its side. "Happy?"

Kiin shook her head, then looked at Markus. "Could you help with the fire?"

Markus happily produced his wand and was about to use the spell he knew best, then a little wisdom entered his mind, and he set the wand down, allowing it to fade away. He considered the last time he had used the wand to cast that spell. Blowing up the pile of wood with an explosive ball of flames might not be the best idea. He held out his hand and said, "Eldr."

A little flame shot at the grass and brush used for kindling under the wood. It lit up instantly, and Kiin went to work, managing it into a good campfire.

"Yeah, that's a good idea. Use magic," Treb mumbled as he used his knife to begin the cleaning process.

Markus let out a sigh and figured he was never going to get on this man's good side. He wanted to remind Treb that he had helped save Kiin from the imp attack, and had offered to help him free his people from prison by going on this dangerous quest. But it would probably do little good. Knowing the two of them would take care of the dinner, Markus opened the Codex again and started looking

129

through it. He had hoped to figure something out by now, but it was still just gibberish. However, it did provide something for him to do, so he didn't have to sit there and quietly wait while Treb gave him mean looks.

Markus sat on the log with nothing to do or say. Treb was wrapping the rest of the deer meat into some cloth so they could have it to eat the next few days. The way he ripped the meat apart with his bare hands sent chills down Markus' spine. Was Treb thinking about someone he would like to rip apart like that?

Once Treb had finished packing away the meat, he pulled out his map. It was a basic map of Gallenor that did not show the location of the Citadel, but it did show him where they were and where they were going.

Markus waited for something to come to mind so he might open up a pleasant dialog between them. But, there was simply nothing he could talk about. So, he pulled out the Codex again and opened it. He flipped page after page and looked at it intensely, trying his best to make sense of anything. However, the only sense he could make of it was that some pages had spells, while others just had a lot of words. Spells were written differently, though he could have been wrong about that. After turning the book upside down, holding a page up so the light could shine through it, and even looking at the edges of the pages, Markus shook his head and turned it to the last pages that showed him where to go. At least he understood *this* page.

Looking up, he peered through the trees to see the silhouettes of hills in the distance and he knew there was a river they had followed on the far side of the road near the forest. After gauging the few landmarks around them, he turned again to the map inside the book. He wanted to see if he could figure out where they were. He found the river and hills, but the way they were drawn did not show him his precise whereabouts. It really didn't matter. Until they got to the mountains in the north, Treb's map was far superior. But Markus pretended to be focused on his work.

Once Markus tired of holding the big book, he closed it and set it down. He looked at the stars and realized something. "What time is it?" he quietly asked.

Treb looked up and then shrugged. "Probably eight hours till sunrise."

"Oh, so it's not quite midnight yet. Oh, well, it really doesn't matter anyway." He was talking to himself more than to Treb.

Treb frowned. "What are you going on about?"

Markus smiled. "It's my birthday. I almost forgot. I turned sixteen today. I had always looked forward to this birthday, and here it is, and I'm sitting on the forest floor, practically alone."

Treb let out a sigh. "What did you expect on your sixteenth birthday?"

Markus smiled at the stars. "I had expected to be heading into school to become a wizard. I thought I might even be searching for a mentor to apprentice under. It was to be the start of my new life, a life where I would be a man who brought good things to my home and made everyone's life easier. Maybe even a party with friends. I never expected this."

Treb's sour attitude melted a little, and he set aside his map for the moment. "I'm sorry your birthday didn't live up to your expectations. When Crystal turned sixteen a month ago, we gave her a great party."

Markus took the opportunity to say something in an effort to change their relationship. "Look, I'm sorry if I got between you and your daughter." It was a total change of subject, but he wanted to say it while he had the courage to.

Treb was surprised and shocked. "What?"

"I know you love her and she loves you. And you would do anything to protect her and make her happy. When I met her, I found a friend, and she seemed to like me back. You can't blame a guy for liking a pretty girl who wants to be around him. But if I'd known how it would make you feel, I wouldn't have let her put me between you guys."

"Listen, Markus, I'm . . ." Treb took a moment to swallow his pride. "I'm sorry if I made you feel uncomfortable. It was mean of me to act so possessive of her. She is my little girl and . . . well . . . I wanted to keep her safe. The truth is, she hasn't really ever responded to any of the flirts around the village, and that sort of made me comfortable knowing she was kept safe from a broken heart. When she immediately took to you, I got . . . I guess . . . I got jealous. My little girl was acting like a young lady, and that scared this dad to death. You didn't mean to scare me, and it's good she wants to be around boys her own age."

Markus joked, "It's about time."

Treb got up and walked over to Markus and sat next to him on the log, in almost the same place that Kiin had sat earlier. "You're an honorable person—at least, so far. You're risking your life for people you don't know. Not just the Rakki, but everyone. I should respect you for that; not hold a grudge. Is there anything I can do to make your birthday any better? What's left of it, that is?"

Markus smiled at Treb. "Well, since it's just you and me, maybe you could help me with something."

"What?"

"Could you tell me about girls?" Markus asked quickly and with an eager smile.

Treb frowned as he leaned back, fearful of having *that* conversation. "Uh . . . didn't your father already talk to you about the . . . uh . . . facts of life?"

Markus laughed nervously. "Oh, I know all about that. What I want to know is: how do you get a date? I . . . well . . . I mean to say, I didn't have a lot of time to date and whatnot back at my village, and my father hardly talked about anything but the farm, so I don't know a lot about asking a girl out—what to do on a date, what not to do."

"I'm honored you would ask me, but what makes you think I know all of that?"

"Well, you have a smart, savvy, beautiful wife, and have raised a nice teenage girl. You must know a few things." It was unintentional flattery.

Treb laughed and agreed with a nod. "I guess—when you put it that way. I do know a few things about women. First thing, as a guy, you'll never fully understand them. Just realize that. Next, understand they aren't boys; they're the opposite sex. Focus on the opposite part. After that . . ."

As the night continued, Treb and Markus talked for some time about this subject. Markus was greedily eating it up while Treb warmed up to the boy.

From where she had been sitting, Kiin could hear a little of what they were talking about, and she would probably have to correct her husband on a few points later. But she smiled warmly at the sight of the two finally hitting it off. It saddened her to think that Treb was truly a good father, a man who could raise a girl or boy with skill, but would never have one of his own with whom to do so.

Kiin had listened long enough, having waited for almost two hours while the two chatted. It was time to get to bed, and she knew that her husband could talk the ears off anything once he got started.

"Well, you two seem to have gotten over the uncomfortable silence," Kiin said loudly to give them a little warning of her approach.

Treb turned around with a guilty smile, knowing if she had heard some of his advice for dealing with mood swings, he could be sleeping at his mother's when they got back home. "Oh, hi, honey."

Markus nodded. "Treb and I are friends now. And he was just telling me all sorts of great stuff." He knew better than to go into detail from the look Treb gave him.

Kiin knelt down and poked the fire to get it heated up. "What sort of stuff?" She played ignorant for their benefit.

Treb said, "Hunting imps," while at the same time, Markus said,

"Cooking."

"You know, hunting and cooking an imp will give you one heck of a sour stomach," she teased.

Markus stood up and stretched. His whole body felt the effects of sitting for several hours on a log. "Well, I think I'm ready for bed. I'm tired." He started to yawn and suddenly felt Treb's hand push him down. "Hey, what . . ." He then noticed that both Kiin and Treb had their bows out and were looking into the trees for something.

"Did you hear it?" Treb asked his wife.

She gave a short nod. "Yes, the buzzing."

Suddenly a green imp came flying through the forest and shot a bolt of red energy at the campfire, which caused it to burst all over the place and forced the two warriors to dance around to avoid being burned.

"Damned mischievous imp!" Treb growled out and quickly regained his posture with his bow.

Just then, the imp flew by again, and with a wicked little cackle, it threw a green ball of gas at them, which exploded across the ground and smelled perfectly horrible. Treb shot at the little beast, but only hit a tree. Kiin followed his arrow with one of her own, and she shot the creature in the wings. The imp crashed into the ground.

"Did you see where it landed?" Treb scanned the area, another arrow pulled back next to his cheek, by his eye.

Kiin looked, but did not see the imp. "Damn."

"I'll take that as a no. Wait, I heard something . . ." Treb pointed his arrow in the tufts of grass behind where Markus had been sitting.

Kiin leveled her arrow the other direction at a bush. "I hear something over here." Suddenly, she saw a flash. "It's casting!"

With a quick double snap of bowstrings, both Treb and Kiin released their arrows at their targets. Where Kiin had shot, there was a blast of energy and she grinned.

"Got it," she said upon hearing the imp exploding.

Treb's target did not explode; it screamed and then cried. "What on earth?"

Markus looked up at the worried Rakki. "Can I get up now?"

Treb nodded. "Yes. Oh, no! I think I hit someone."

Kiin knocked an arrow to her bow and pointed it at the location of his last shot. "Whoever you are, show yourself!"

All three paused. The crackle of the fire and the sound of pitiful crying was all that could be heard.

Suddenly, Treb's eyes widened and he threw his bow away. "Crystal!" His Rakki ears had finally determined the familiarity of the crying. He bounded over the log and then dove through the grass.

"Oh no!"

Kiin threw her bow too, and followed her husband. "Crystal!?"

Markus ran after them, not sure how they could possibly know who it was, or why Crystal would be out there. But, sure enough, there she lay with an arrow sticking out of her shoulder. She was curled up with her knees to her chest and her left hand holding her shoulder where the blood was soaking her fur. She had tears running down her face while she cried with a weak whimper.

"Crystal? What's she doing out here?" Markus asked.

Kiin shook her head. "I don't know."

Treb knelt down and picked her up as gently as he could and carried her back to their camp.

"Kiin! Help me!" Treb called out, a pained desperation in his voice.

Kiin looked at the arrow and even touched it once to see where it was. This made Crystal cry out. Kiin spoke calmly. "Treb, the arrow has met bone. We cannot push it through; it'll have to be pulled out."

"What?!" Crystal cried, terrified at the thought.

Treb held in his own urge to tear up and softly said, "Kiin, please hold her while I do this."

Kiin came over and held Crystal. "Honey, your father has to pull out the arrow. It's going to hurt, but it'll feel better when he's done."

Crystal was fighting through her tears, but she nodded.

Treb bit his lip and carefully twisted the arrow for the best position to pull from. Then, with a hard yank, he freed it from her arm. Markus cringed, and Crystal let out a yelp that sounded a little more canine than human.

Treb tossed the arrow into the fire. "It's out. Now I have to bind it."

"No," Crystal managed to say.

"Honey, I have to bind it or it'll get infected and could get worse," Treb pleaded with her.

"Father . . ." She strained under the pain surging through her arm. "I have something that'll help. Markus."

Markus quickly stepped over to her. "What?"

"My bag—get my book." With her good arm, she pointed back to where she had been crouching all this time.

Markus did not question her and ran back to where there was still blood on the ground. There was also a little bag. Inside was a small book that she wrote her medical spells into. With the bag and book in hand, he ran back. "I have it."

"Page two," she said through clinched teeth.

Markus turned to the second page and found a spell with a short description in her handwriting. "Okay. Is this all there is to it?"

She nodded. "Yes, it's a simple healing spell, but if you focus your mind and use that wand of yours, you can heal deep wounds like this."

Markus was nervous, but he trusted her wisdom. "Wand!" he called out, and his wand appeared. Then he came down to one knee, right next to her, opposite a frightened Treb. Markus pointed the wand at her shoulder and closed his eyes. "Asja." The wand flashed with blue light and worked for a moment.

Crystal recoiled when the spell stopped working and the pain returned. "Keep saying it; you have to keep saying it."

Markus felt stupid. He knew that was how some spells worked. So, he started again. "Asja . . . Asja . . . Asja . . . " As soon as the spell started to fluctuate, he would say it again, and the magic continued. Crystal's body would heal itself, but the spell accelerated the rate by an enormous amount. With one last "Asja," the opening in her arm closed and sealed, as though nothing had ever happened, though the blood soaking her fur remained.

Treb quickly asked, "Crystal, are you okay? Did it work?"

Crystal gave her father the same smile she always used when he was being overly worried about her. "It worked fine. I feel better. Please help me up."

Treb sat back and held out his hands to her and gave her every bit of support he could. Once she got to her feet, she sat back down on the log. The pain was only in her mind now, but the freshness of the memory made her continue to hold her arm.

Markus stood when she got up and looked around with a forced smile. Everything was all right now. Crystal was not harmed anymore, and the imp attack was over. "I'm glad you had that spell," he told her.

Crystal smiled back at him. "I'm glad you were able to cast it."

Then Treb started, "What are you doing here!?" The angry father in him now burst out.

Kiin took his hand. "Honey, calm down." She looked at Crystal and asked again, "Dear, what were you doing in the brush behind us?"

"How long have you been following us?!" Treb bellowed before Crystal had a chance to answer.

Crystal gulped and looked down, unable to look them in the eyes. "I . . . I have been, uh, following you since, well, you left."

Treb huffed loudly. "That was two days ago! We've traveled a full five widths! What were you thinking?!"

Kiin grabbed his tail and yanked it hard enough to force him to stand behind her. She glared at him and said, "Don't yell!"

"But—!" he argued and pointed at their daughter, only to be stopped by the look in his wife's eyes. He might have been a big, muscled, ferocious Rakki warrior, but his wife could put real fear into him.

Kiin cleared her throat, turned around, and calmly, yet directly, asked, "What gave you the notion to follow us?"

Crystal still did not look up at them. "I . . . I wanted . . . to see my parents again. I thought I could . . . I thought . . . I don't know what I was thinking." She kept holding her shoulder.

"Did you plan on telling us you were coming along? Or were you going to just track us the whole way?"

"Uh . . . I . . . I don't know."

Kiin put her hands on her hips and shook her head. "You don't know. Do you realize how stupid this was? What if that arrow had hit you in the heart? What if an imp found you? Did you bring enough food? Did you have any idea where we're going? What if you lost us?"

Crystal was on the verge of crying again. "I . . . I don't know." Tears fell down her face. "I just couldn't stand watching you leave; you're all I have left. If I came along, I would still be with you, and eventually see my real parents again, too."

Kiin's anger subsided slightly and she knelt down in front of Crystal and lifted her tear-streaked face. "Honey, I know how much pain you've been in over the past four years, but this was a foolish thing to do. You could've gotten yourself into much more trouble than you already did."

Crystal put her arms around her mother and cried. "I'm sorry! I didn't mean to make you so mad at me."

Kiin hugged her back. "We aren't mad, just displeased with your poor choice of actions. You're smarter than this." They stayed together for a long time.

Treb stepped over and let out a softer sigh. "Honey, I didn't mean to yell at you. I'm just angry that you put yourself in such a dangerous position."

Crystal leaned back and looked at her father, the fur on her face wet from tears. "I'm sorry. Am I in a lot of trouble?"

Treb smiled and shook his head. "No, I suppose hitting you with an arrow is punishment enough."

Kiin stood up and cocked her head when she heard Crystal's stomach growling. "What did you bring to eat?"

Crystal showed them the stale bread. "This. And some nuts."

Kiin walked around and plopped a large piece of wood on the fire.

"Treb, get out some of the meat and heat it up."

Treb nodded and went to unbind a portion of the cooked deer.

Markus smiled and walked over to the log. He sat down next to her. "I'm glad I could help you."

Crystal wiped her face. "You did great. I have something for you." She reached into the bottom of her little bag and pulled out a handful of copper coins. She placed them in his hand. "You dropped these."

Markus laughed. "So, it was you we heard behind us."

"Here." Treb came back over with a cloth in his hands filled with some of the meat.

Crystal took it with an eager grin. "Wow, this smelled so good when you were cooking it."

Kiin rolled out her bed. "You can sleep on my mat tonight."

Markus decided it was a good time to be gallant. "No, she can use mine, and I can sleep on the forest floor."

"No, Treb and I will be taking turns on lookout. That imp will probably not be the last. We'll just trade off on the mat. You two can rest all night."

Treb cleared his throat and looked at the mats. "Honey, why don't you put yours on the other side of the fire." He didn't like seeing Crystal and Markus' beds right next to each other.

Kiin smiled at him. She knew exactly what he was doing. "Fine." She dragged the mat over to the other side of the fire and laid it out. "You'll sleep here, Crystal."

Markus stood up and walked over to his mat. "Goodnight, all. I'm worn out."

Treb and Kiin quietly finished getting the camp ready for the night, and then Treb took the next watch. Markus and Crystal slept with both the fire and one adult between them.

CHAPTER 9: THE ENCOUNTER

THE next morning, Markus helped Crystal roll up the mats and prepare the packs for all three to carry. Crystal had only brought with her a small bag with her book and some food in it, so she did not have a large pack. Treb and Kiin were off in the distance having a discussion, which seemed to worry Crystal. Markus had gotten used to the two of them speaking privately.

Crystal saw that Markus had placed the Codex under his pillow. "Why was that there? Keeping it safe?"

"Partly. I was also hoping to dream about it, maybe see some answers about reading it."

"Did it work?"

He shook his head. "It is strange. But since I started this journey, the dreams have come to a stop. The last one I had was during the only night I spent in your village, and that might've been just a regular dream with magic in it."

"Is that a bad sign?"

"I don't know. It doesn't answer the questions about my dreams and what they mean. I'm still searching for that."

"I see." Though she answered him, Crystal's attention was

diverted.

Markus could see that she was worried and wanted to ease her tension. "Crystal, did you ever read about the Great War in that huge library of yours?"

"Yes. In fact, some of the most inclusive manuscripts from the historians of that age are stored at the library."

"I think there isn't anything that library of yours doesn't have. We had a small shop that was turned into a library some time back. I learned a little about the Great War from the old books, but not much."

"What do you want to know?"

"I never learned what started the War and why there were dragons."

Crystal started in, recalling the text as best as she could. "There were nine dragons. The dragons were actually wizards who were changed into dragons. When one of the nine died of old age and a new seat was opened, another wizard was made a dragon, somehow. Only great and honorable wizards were allowed to become dragons."

Markus frowned. "How do you change into a dragon?"

"I don't know. That information wasn't in any text."

Markus smiled at her. "So, not everything is in that library of yours."

"Well, I haven't read everything." She grinned at him, and then continued. "The wizards started coming to our lands and marrying our people. For some reason, this angered the wizards back in their own lands and it started a conflict that turned into a civil war. It spilled over to our lands, and our people were forced to choose a side. We sided with the Dragon Council and the wizards who supported it."

Markus cocked his head. "What happened next?"

"No one knows for sure. With some kinda great spell, the dragons were destroyed, but so were the enemies of the wizards. The ancient wizards were all destroyed, and only their children, in our lands, survived. Some say the dragons sacrificed themselves to save us, while others believe it was dark wizards who cast a foolish spell, dooming all of the ancients. All that's known is the ancient wizards were destroyed in one day."

"Not all of them," Markus stated quietly.

"Huh?"

Markus held out his hand and the wand appeared. "The wizard who gave me this said he was an Ancient. Probably the last one left living in Gallenor."

Crystal was in awe. "Wow. To have spoken with an Ancient.

That's amazing."

Markus tossed the wand away; it vanished just before it hit the ground. "I barely had time to ask him anything except why he would want me to take on such a mission."

"What did he say?"

Markus shook his head. "I don't believe he chose me specifically. He just needed someone who didn't have an agenda, one way or another, who was willing to take this foolish mission."

Crystal solemnly stated, "This foolish mission will bring back my parents."

Markus realized how stupid his comment was. "Oh, I didn't mean it that way. I just . . . wasn't thinking. It's a great mission; I just don't think I'm the best choice for it." He gave her a confident grin. "But, I'll do everything I can to complete it."

"Thanks."

Just then, Treb and Kiin came back. "So, is everything ready to go?" Kiin asked.

Markus and Crystal stood up. Crystal still acted very guilty around them, but Markus was more eager. He pointed to the perfectly packed bags. "Yup."

"All right." Treb grabbed a bag and started to put it over his shoulders. "I'll take this one. Kiin and Crystal, you each take the other two."

Markus grabbed the one Crystal had already put her hand on. "No, I can carry this."

Kiin shook her head and put her bag on. "No, Crystal's coming with me. You two will head for the Citadel. I'm taking her home."

"No!" Crystal yelled at them, then shut her mouth tight. She had never yelled at her parents. And it scared her to think she had just done that.

Treb did not become angry; he had expected her to resist. "Crystal, this isn't a safe mission. I don't want you in harm's way. You'll be safe at the village with Kiin."

Crystal looked as though she were about to cry. "I have to go with you. This is too important. I want to help free my parents."

Kiin took Crystal's hand. "Honey, we've already discussed this, and I'm not going to listen to your arguments. We're going home."

Markus wanted to say something in Crystal's defense, because he really wanted her to come with them. But he understood her parents' reasoning and knew better than to get into a family issue. He had just gotten on Treb's good side; he didn't want to ruin that so soon.

Treb broke the silence as he started to walk away. "Come on, we need to get on the road."

The other three quietly followed him out of the thicket of trees and headed for the little dirt road that would direct Kiin and Crystal back toward the village.

"Hey, what am I going to sleep on for the rest of this trip?" Markus asked as they walked down the hill toward the road.

Treb pointed off toward the north. "We'll get to Stillwater by nightfall, and there we can purchase some more supplies for the road."

Crystal protested one last time as she saw the road where they would depart from the others. "I can take care of myself. I'm sixteen now. And you could use the medical magic I know."

Treb turned to her, about to hotly explain himself again, but Kiin came up from behind her and held her shoulders. "Honey, please don't fight this. Just tell him goodbye and we can go home."

Markus looked up and saw what seemed to be a dirt cloud rising up on the road, down the hill from where they were standing, but he didn't say anything just yet.

Treb nodded at Crystal. "Listen to her. Trust me. I only do this because I love you."

Kiin pushed Crystal towards Treb. "Give him a hug."

Crystal knew he loved her, which was the reason behind what he was doing. So, she put her arms around him and gave him a great hug. "I do love you, Daddy."

He hugged her back. "So do I. I'll come home as quickly as possible, and I'll be bringing your real parents with me."

"Uh . . . what's that?" Markus interrupted.

Treb looked up from hugging Crystal to see several Royal Guards come racing down the road. "Trouble."

Kiin cleared her throat and quietly stated, "Stay calm. Perhaps they'll just pass us."

Treb held his daughter's shoulders and walked with her to the north, acting as though they were simply on their way. Kiin walked on her other side, keeping between the passing Guards and her daughter. Markus stayed on Treb's far side, putting all three of his companions between him and the Guard's eyes.

"HALT!" yelled Captain Morris as he turned his horse and ran up the short hill toward the Rakki and the human. Two of his fellow Guards followed along.

Treb gritted his teeth and stopped. He and Kiin turned so they were in front of Crystal and Markus. The three men on horses surrounded them, the Guards with their swords drawn.

Treb had his bow in his hand, but it was not yet ready to fire, as he didn't want to provoke anything. He smiled at them and asked, "How can we help you today?"

Morris glared at them. "I'm searching for any wizards. By order of King Anthony, they are to be apprehended for the good of Gallenor."

Markus became very nervous and looked at Crystal. In a hushed voice, he said, "That's the guy who was after Tolen." Crystal's eyes turned wide and she started to shake. Markus took her hand and tried to help calm her down. Looking scared was the worst kind of incrimination right now.

Kiin shifted position a few times to keep Morris' line of sight away from the kids behind her. "Well, I'm afraid we cannot oblige today. None of us are wizards, just travelers."

Morris sneered in disbelief. "What are you doing out here, so far from the Rakki village? What are you doing with a Humankind?"

"We're hunting imps." Treb glowered at Morris. "They're plaguing our people, and the Royal Armies have stopped keeping the imp population under control."

Kiin added, "And since when is it a crime to have a Humankind with us? All the races are free to be together in friendship—or have the equality laws been repealed?"

"I'm the law in Gallenor. If I decide you should go home, you'll go home. If I decide you need to spend a little time in prison, you will. Do not get haughty with me."

Treb snarled, but contained his growling. "Well, then, unless you need to imprison us, we really need to be on our way, as I'm sure you need to go as well."

Morris sat up on his horse and nodded to his men. "Fine. Be on your way, but just be careful . . ."

"Sir!" One of his men pointed at the little satchel hanging from his horse.

Morris looked down and an evil grin spread across his face. He reached down and retrieved a red glowing stone. "Well, well, well. It appears there *is* a wizard in our presence."

In a fraction of a second, Treb picked up his bow, pulled out an arrow, and had it ready to fire an inch away from Morris' head. He then growled out at Morris, "You won't live to lay one single finger on my daughter!"

The two Guards immediately pulled out their swords, and Kiin produced an arrow as well, shifting her aim between the guards. Everyone was on high tension, even Morris.

The captain held up his hands. "You loose that arrow, and the entire legion under the King will hunt you down and skin that fur hide off of your body."

Crystal was squeezing Markus' hand, scared to death. She managed to whisper to him, "Stop them." There was a strange, awful fear in her eyes. She was staring at Morris as though he were a massive demon.

Markus understood how terrified she was and that Treb's arrow could bring about a terrible fight. So, he came up with a brilliant solution. With a single thought, he produced his wand. Then he let go of Crystal's hand and ran back a few steps, "Hey, you want a wizard? Here I am!" He showed them his wand.

"It's the boy! Get him!" Morris yelled at his men.

Markus grinned and then waved the wand around his head, finishing with a snapping point into the sky. A stream of fire came flowing off the end of the wand, and it turned into a torrent of flames. The flames grew and grew, forming a huge blazing bird, rising into the sky. The bird let out a shrill, echoing scream, and proceeded to fly down, going directly for the soldiers. Markus was in awe of what he was doing. The spell was the same one he had read in the Rakki library. He didn't say the words, but rather thought of what he wanted, and the bird came. In a strange way, he was controlling it with his emotions, and it felt really good.

The soldiers were shocked and stopped their attack. Their horses were scared to death. One reared up, nearly throwing its rider, and the other horse turned and ran as if its master had just spurred it with razor blades. The first horse followed behind quickly, their riders at the animals' mercy.

The firebird flew right at Morris, as it was directed by Markus' will. Morris wasn't as scared of it as his men, but his horse was less courageous in the face of this flame demon. The frightened horse almost kicked Treb in the face while it found the quickest path away from the approaching monster. Morris was at his horse's whim and was taken away with the firebird close behind him.

Both Treb and Kiin dove to the ground so as not to be hit by the bird that was heading for them. Crystal didn't budge. She smiled while the orange, flaming beast flew right through her and continued toward the fleeing soldiers.

"Mom, Dad, it's fake. Just an illusion."

Markus, who was still controlling the bird, ran back down the hill at them. "And, it won't last long. We really should get away from here—*now*!" He started running northward.

Treb and Kiin scrambled to their feet. Treb grabbed Crystal's hand and ran with her. Kiin kept her bow in hand as she followed her husband and daughter. If the men came back for either Crystal or Markus, she would see to it they knew her arrows were no illusion.

Markus could no longer see his creation and let it go. It would dissipate within a few minutes, and the Guards would realize it was a ruse. By that time, hopefully, the trio would be long gone.

Captain Morris forced his horse to come to a skidding stop. "Stop, you fools!" The other two Guards stopped their horses and turned around. Morris looked back. "The firebird's gone; it was an illusion. That damned kid fooled us."

The two Guards then trotted back up to him. One asked, "What now?"

The Captain was grinding his teeth. No one made a fool of Morris and got away from him. "This wizard child is trying to run from us. I won't allow it."

"Should we go after them?"

"No." His answer came out a bit slow, a pondering look in his eyes. He quickly came up with a plan and gave his orders. "I'll go alone for now. Trent, head back to the Capital and tell the King that there's at least one rogue wizard child. Chris, head back to the Rakki village and tell Kellus that two of his noble Arrowguard soldiers are aiding and abetting criminals."

Chris frowned. "How do you know those Rakki are part of the Rakki Arrowguard?"

Morris looked back in the direction they had been running. "The male bore the symbol of the Arrowguard on his armor. The Rakki are a proud and noble people. It would be against all of their codes of conduct to wear such a symbol without earning it. Those two answer to Kellus, and Kellus will answer to me if he allowed them to do this." He turned sharply and pointed at Chris. "Tell the dog king that the King of Gallenor will annex his forest and put all of his people in chains if he's part of this."

"Sir?" Both men were shocked at the relentless attitude of their leader.

Morris turned his horse to start heading back. "The laws of the King supersede any local authority. To violate them is dangerous. Remind Kellus of that. I'll head for Stillwater, as I'm sure those people will need to stop there for fresh supplies. From there, I'll send a hawk back to Thendor with further instructions. Now, get to your duties!" he yelled as he charged his horse away from them.

"Aye, sir." Both loyal subordinates saluted their commander.

"I can't keep running. My legs hurt," Crystal whimpered.

Treb stopped dragging her and paused for everyone to catch their breath. Markus and Crystal were much more out of breath than Kiin or Treb, but all their muscles ached from dashing for the last hour.

Kiin leaned on Treb. "That man—he won't stop hunting us."

"That's Captain Morris, isn't it?" Markus asked while he held his knees to catch his breath.

Treb stuck up one eyebrow. "Yes. How do you know him?"

Markus stood up and stretched his back. "When Tolen gave me the wand and the mission, that man showed up with his soldiers. I hid when he questioned Tolen. For some reason, he'd been searching for Tolen for a long time."

Kiin frowned. "Did they get Tolen? Is he trapped in the Labyrinth?"

"Tolen died," Markus stated plainly. "He was very old and hardly able to speak to me. I don't know how he managed to stay alive long enough for me to find him, but he died only moments after he gave me the mission. That Morris guy must've been searching for Tolen like he's looking for us—to imprison wizards."

Treb shook his head. "No, Morris was searching for Tolen because the King wanted Tolen specifically. Back when they first took our wizards, they gave us a decree from the King. If Tolen the Wise was found on our lands, he was to be turned over to the King immediately. Tolen was the only wizard searched for like that."

Markus thought about Treb's revelation. "It *did* seem odd the way Morris acted around Tolen when they spoke. It was as though Tolen was keeping something from Morris and from the King. My guess is that it had something to do with the Citadel and the Dragonwand."

Kiin walked past Markus, up the hill a little ways. "Then we need to get there first." She went up a bit higher than the others and

159

looked out over the distant road.

Treb came over to Crystal, who was still shaken. "Are you okay?" he asked.

She was looking off in the distance, seemingly lost in a memory. "It was him," she whispered.

Treb frowned. "Who?"

"That man—the one you pointed your arrow at—that's the man who took my parents." She was shaking all over, panic taking over her mind.

Treb then realized it indeed had been Captain Morris who had come to their house and picked up Shio and Fiona, Crystal's parents. All of the other Guards under his command had gone around, capturing the others, and Morris had been arresting the last two. "It was. I'd forgotten."

It was clear from Crystal's face that every ounce of control in her was being used to restrain the need to cry. "I was so scared when I saw his face. I knew he'd come for me. He was going to take me away."

Treb took her in his arms, and she buried her face in his shoulder, crying. He brushed his hand down the back of her head. "Oh, my precious little girl. I would never let him take you away. I would rather die than see that happen."

She cried, "I don't want to go home! He'll find me there!" The sound of her voice was muffled against Treb's body, but even Markus could understand what she had said.

Treb closed his eyes and rested his head down on hers. "No, I can't send you home now. He'll look for you there. You'll come with us."

Crystal started bawling. "Don't let him take me. Don't let him take me."

Watching her, Markus felt really awkward. He realized before how horrible it was that her parents had been taken from her. But he had not come face to face with the reality of how deep her fear was until that moment. Had he not known to use that illusion spell, those Guards could have cut down her adopted parents in front of her, and then taken her and him away to prison. Her world would have been destroyed in a few moments. His heart swelled, and his own eyes filled with tears—not for his own safety, but for hers.

"Move! He's coming!" Kiin ran back down the hill, pushing everyone to get behind a large rock.

As Markus headed for the rock, he saw that there was one man riding furiously down the dirt road. Morris was still after them. For a brief moment, Markus considered using his spell again, but logically, Morris would be wise to it, and it would only give away their position. So he jumped behind the rock and pressed himself up

161

against it with Crystal right next to him. Treb and Kiin both held their bows with arrows at the ready.

"Crystal, quiet down, please," Kiin whispered.

Crystal was so scared, she was having a hard time controlling herself. Her whimpering and hard breathing might have alerted Captain Morris to their location.

Markus took her and held her against him. He used his body to muffle the sounds she was making, his hand brushing down the back of her head and her back. He was quietly whispering, "It's going to be all right. Calm down. I won't leave you alone."

Kiin had her eyes glued on the man riding past them. He was oblivious to their presence.

Treb looked over to the children. He was a little surprised at the way Markus was helping Crystal. It was sweet and exactly what she needed right now. He would've been incensed a day ago to see Markus' arms all over her, but right then, he wasn't angry at all. Treb heard Markus say something that helped him understand the boy better.

"Don't worry; I'll let them take me first. You've been hurt too much. I can't allow them to hurt you again," Markus said to Crystal.

Kiin lowered her bow. "We're clear." She looked back at her husband. "Treb? What is it?"

He was still watching Markus and Crystal. Looking back at his wife, he smiled. "Nothing. Just saw something I didn't expect to see."

Crystal leaned back from Markus. "Thanks, I needed that." She wiped her eyes with the back of her hand.

Markus smiled at her, feeling proud of his chivalry. "Glad I could help."

Kiin got up and slung her bow around to her back. "Come on, we need to get moving."

Everyone stood up and looked around to make sure that no one else was behind Morris. Treb turned to his wife. "Where can we go now?"

"Stillwater."

"But, won't Morris be heading there too?" Markus asked.

Kiin nodded. "That'd be my best guess. But we can't go far without resupplying, and with a new person in this group, we don't have enough."

Treb let out a sigh and reluctantly nodded. "Stillwater it is."

"Wait, wait, wait," Markus interjected. "If that Morris is heading for Stillwater, won't he see us there?"

"Stillwater's a big place," Kiin answered. "The guard station is right near the main entrance, and that's where Morris will likely go. There's a smaller, older entrance near the riverfront on the opposite side. We can get in, get our stuff, and leave before Morris has any idea we were there."

Treb nodded. "Sounds like a plan. Now, we need to get moving if we're going to get there through these trees."

They headed off toward the old city of Stillwater, paralleling the road through the trees. Fortunately for them, most imps detested the sunlight and avoided daytime. But this did not mean that Treb or Kiin were any less watchful for possible imp attacks. Markus walked close to Crystal, doing his best to get her to smile and not think about the overwhelming fear that bubbled in her belly.

CHAPTER 10: INTO STILLWATER

THE city of Stillwater was the third largest city in Gallenor. Thendor was the largest, and the Port of Pearls was the second, but this did not make Stillwater any less proud. The city was considered one of the oldest, and it had once belonged to a long forgotten empire that stretched into the lands before they were called Gallenor.

The stark, barren lands of the desolate mountains and wastes to the north offset the lush green grasses and forests of the lands south of Stillwater. The land then turned into sharp peaks without much vegetation. Stillwater was settled on a river that provided the weary travelers water before they headed north. Past the desolate mountains and wastes were the sheer cold lands of the far north. No one traveled these lands, and only the heartiest of animals lived there.

Stillwater had been built long ago on the river. The thick stone buildings and decaying fort at the south entrance displayed its history well. From there, the city grew with each passing generation. The buildings changed from thicker stone to a smaller, yet just as sturdy manmade stone. Then wood buildings and metal structures came in, and finally, when Gallenor decided to make the city a central outpost for the Royal Guard, a wall had been constructed around it.

The wall that Gallenor constructed was actually only two thirds of a wall; one third of it was the ancient wall when the city had been a fortress. A testament to the construction of the forgotten empire, the still used part of the wall stood stronger than the other two thirds built by Gallenor. It had taken a massive fight between dragons to destroy part of the ancient wall, and even that hadn't completely taken it down.

History was not on the mind of Stillwater's local potion vendor this evening. Donna was the local apothecary and as such, she was always needed. When a child scraped his arm or bumped his head, parents would come running for one of her famous pain relief potions. She sold potions that could cure most illnesses, season food, and even protect a garden from imps. Yes, she was a popular vendor in Stillwater, and the money was always welcomed. The only potion she did not sell was the infamous love potion. It did exist, but it was nothing more than an infatuation potion that was illegal to brew and foolish to take. However, some days, poor Donna considered it an option because she was single and always looking. But from behind the stand where she sold her potions, most men did not look for love. They just wanted a bargain.

"Ms. Donna, Ms. Donna!" a young boy cried, running up to her. He was a human child with sandy blonde hair and dirt on just about every part of his body.

She stepped out from behind the stand and knelt down. "And what does little Trevor want today?"

Trevor held up a sagging mess of what looked like a thin bag. "Um . . . do you have it—the floating potion?"

"Now, Trevor, you know that I sell these potions. I don't always give them away." She was teasing him.

He pouted and just about cried. "But, Daddy just got this for me and, and, and I thought you could make it float." He held it up for her.

She took it from him and looked at his prize. It was a sheep's stomach that had been extracted from one of his father's butcherings that afternoon. "All right, just this once," she said.

Of course, once had been four times this week already. But she always liked the way it made him happy. The stomach had been tied off at one end, and there was an opening at the other. She searched through her more magical potions and found a white sparkling one that was not commonly sold to just any customer. Donna pulled the cork out and then carefully tipped it up and put three drops into the stomach. Quickly, she pinched the open end closed, and then got a little string from her stand and tied it off. "Here you go," she said, handing it back to him.

Trevor took the limp stomach and waited eagerly as it swelled up with magical gas. Soon, it was so round and tight, it looked as though it would burst with one tap against a moderately sharp object. He let go of it, and it floated up a little and then hung in the air only four feet off of the ground. "WHOO-HOOO!" he yelled out, and then batted it down the street, directing it to a group of his friends who would use it to invent yet another sport with a hovering, inflated sheep stomach.

"Donna, you're too nice. That's a special potion, and you're just giving it away," an older woman said, coming up to the booth.

"What use does an old flotation potion have for me otherwise? No one will buy it any time soon. Besides, that kind of potion costs a lot more than anyone around here has to spend."

The older woman, Marguerite, laughed and shook her head. "But every time one of the Guards sees that kind of potion, they send someone over to see if you're a wizard."

"Yeah, you'd think that after the thousandth time, they'd get the idea that I'm not a wizard, just an apothecary."

"Well, as you are our local apothecary, I need a potion." Marguerite looked at all the bottles sitting out on display.

Donna gave her friend a very knowing smirk and pulled out a vial of black liquid. "Some spirit remover again?"

Marguerite feigned offense. "What would make you think I needed that?"

Donna cleared her throat. "I wouldn't know."

"Well, since you are offering it, I suppose getting another bottle wouldn't be bad. Of course, what I came for is a bottle of your flower food potion. My roses look a little weak right now."

"Sure, that'll be four coin." Donna picked up a small bottle of the pink liquid she mixed for the flowers, and put it with the black liquid.

Marguerite took out the four silver coins, paid for her products, and placed them in her basket with the two loaves of bread and the freshly plucked and wrapped goose. "That's all. Have a nice day."

Donna smiled and put the coins in her box.

"Oh, Donna, one more thing." Marguerite returned to the booth and leaned over it a little to speak a more privately. "I saw Captain Morris come in to town earlier. If you are going to use that love potion of yours, you had better douse yourself with it now."

Donna rolled her eyes but grinned all the same. "What makes you think I have any love potion?"

"Oh, just like I don't need any spirit remover. Good evening, Donna." Marguerite waved and left for home.

Donna shook her head and walked back from her booth into the building she used to mix her potions. It was funny to her that most people hid their use of spirit remover potions.

She made her way over to a large, ornate cabinet that housed her most special potions. Donna opened the wooden doors and looked upon dozens of bottles in various sizes, each containing numerous potions for all occasions. These were the most expensive and rarest of potions; often, the ingredients were only found in remote locations and from rare things. She reached up and picked up a small teardrop-shaped bottle that was very smooth and filled with a clear liquid. When it hit the light, the liquid had a glow that was golden and pink at the same time. This was a real love potion, one that could cause any man to go crazy for her, at least until the effects wore off. To own the recipe to mix a potion like this was illegal enough, but to actually have the potion was by far even more illegal.

For a terrifically brief moment, she considered the dashingly handsome Captain Morris who was destined to make another stop by her place. *No, it would be foolish, and he, of all people, could lock her up for such a thing*, she thought. She replaced the potion and then took a small wooden box from the back of the cabinet. Using a key tied to a bracelet, she unlocked the box and pulled out a small metal flask. Donna uncorked it, and then dabbed a bit of it on her neck and arms like a woman placing a bit of perfume.

Just then, the door to her place opened, and in strode the

handsome Captain Morris. He flashed his golden grin and walked over to her, his shining armor glinting off a few of the more exotic potions around the place. "Donna the Apothecary, I see you are doing good business."

Donna calmly and discretely placed the flask into the box, locked it, and then closed the cabinet. Turning around to him, she smiled. "Well, if it isn't the gallant Morris come to pay me another visit."

He knew full well she was attracted to him, and he sort of enjoyed toying with her flirtations now and then. Of course, he wasn't ever going to fulfill her fantasy. "It seems yet another local has reported a wizard here. They believe your potions carry a little more than just ingredients. Perhaps a little magic."

Donna cocked her head and grinned at him. "Now, now, Morris, you know we've been through this a dozen times. I pass your test each time you come to town. I'm no more a wizard than you. I just make special things that seem like magic."

Morris cleared his throat and looked around the room. "It does strike me odd that when we apprehended all wizards in Gallenor, almost every apothecary was shut down."

"Ah, but there are others like me. Not all apothecaries are wizards."

He walked around the room, looking at some of the glowing

liquids with a critical gaze. "Yes, but I haven't found one yet with the . . . *uniqueness* of your talents."

"I'll simply take that as a compliment. If you're not convinced that I'm not a wizard, then bring out your stone, and I'll prove it to you once again." Donna held out her arms, waiting for him like she wanted to give him a hug.

He took out the stone and walked around her. This examination took about twice as long as any other he did. There was a part of him that knew she was a wizard; she had to be. Yet, without proof, he could do nothing. So he closed his hand and looked her in the eye. "It seems you're not a wizard today."

"Guess what? I won't be one tomorrow either. Sorry to disappoint you." She gave him a seductive smile. "Now, if you're free tonight, I'd love to use a few of my special cooking potions to make you a fantastic dinner."

Morris put the stone away, ignoring her offer. "So, how did you come by these?" He walked over to a wall with a set of very special potions in slender teardrop shaped bottles.

Donna hid her nervousness well at that moment, for those were a type of magical potion that anyone would recognize. "I keep them on hand for those with the gold to buy them. After all, until the wizards are released, they won't be made again."

Morris slowly reached over and picked up a bottle with a purple potion inside. The frosted smooth glass of the bottle was warm from the magic infused within. "What do they do?" he asked coolly.

Donna could see he was more interested in what these potions did than who made them, so she was in the clear. "Well, Captain, they're unique potions that have powerful abilities. That one is a sleeping potion that can knock out just about anyone. If I'm not mistaken, it was designed by an early wizard apothecary who wanted to stun enemies during the War. The only customers now that have any interest in it are bounty hunters and imp seekers."

Morris twirled the bottle a little, sloshing the liquid around. "So, it can incapacitate an imp. That's impressive. Those creatures are highly resistant to most known stun magic."

Donna leaned up against the counter. She bit her lower lip and bat her eyes, hoping to entice the handsome captain. "You'd be surprised what those potions can do. Just about the only reason potion magic is practiced, with all the available spells, is that it's uniquely powerful. Even a powerful wizard would be taken down by that. For a while, at least. Throw it, and when the bottle breaks, it releases a fog that induces any who breathe it in to sleep."

"What about the user? Wouldn't he be subject to it as well?"

"Yes, unless he drips a single drop of it on his tongue just before using it. That'll give him temporary immunity. Magic potions are complicated pieces of work, but very, very valuable."

Morris gave her the smile every girl in Gallenor loved to see. "I'll take it."

Donna was honestly surprised. "Oh, what would you need with such a potion? All you have to do is charm the imps right out of the sky."

Morris always maintained his focus and attitude, but he did enjoy the way the women responded to him, especially when he had absolutely no intention of indulging them. "Let's just say there are a few rogue wizards the Royal Guards are seeking, and this might help me."

Donna was also practiced at maintaining her attitude, though she despised the idea of helping him to track down and imprison other wizards. Unfortunately for her, if she balked at selling it to him, it might have raised suspicions that could prove difficult to defend. "I hope you understand they are expensive. Not just anyone can afford them."

Morris pulled out a small bag of gold coins and handed it to her. Inside was about twice the value of the potion, but he didn't care. "I'm not just anyone." With that, he walked out of her store, knowing full well she was watching his rear the whole time.

Donna sighed and shook her head. "He needs a good woman.

Someone who would melt that ice in his blood," she stated to no one in particular, and then went back outside to put away her potions and close up shop for the night.

One after another, she put the potion vials into a slotted wooden box designed to carry them. Today had been a good day. She had sold over a hundred potions and made a lot of money.

Suddenly, an odd sound broke her concentration. The old door in the city wall near her shop unlatched. She looked to the side, curious as to whom was using the relic passageway. The ancient door was hardly ever opened, and few travelers came up to this side of the city. There wasn't even a road outside the door any longer. The road had faded into the forest centuries ago.

Three Rakki and a human walked through. The male Rakki nodded to the old City Guard who had opened the door for them.

Donna didn't spend much time wondering who they were worried about seeing; she was too fixed on the big muscles and bare chest of the Rakki warrior. "Wow," she whispered to herself.

CHAPTER 11: FINDING WIZARDS

A young Royal Guard knelt before the Wizard Hallond in his private chambers of the mage tower. The wizard did not look pleased, but outside of public appearances, he never seemed to look happy.

The dutiful soldier began, "Sir, I . . . uh . . . was told to come see you. But, uh, I was supposed to report to the King directly. Captain Morris said that—"

Hallond interrupted him. "Morris knows that I have just as much authority as the King. You can report to me."

"Sir, there was an incident. We have at least one rogue wizard that used a spell to evade us and then fled. We were told to report any runners directly to the King."

Hallond gave the poor young man a grisly smile. "It is all right. You may report to me on this. I am the authority on magic in this kingdom after all. Now, how old is the runner, and what direction was he going?"

"Uh, he looked to be fourteen or fifteen . . . I don't know. He was with several others, and they ran north. Captain Morris is in pursuit and expects to find them in Stillwater."

Hallond calmly asked, "How is it that such a young wizard could use magic powerful enough to make you run? I should think a child would not be so clever, especially against seasoned officers such as yourselves."

"He had a wand and used it to—"

Hallond became very alert just then. "He had a *wand*!? What did it look like?"

"Uh, well . . ." The young soldier had to think hard to recall that exact moment. He had only glanced up at it for a second. "I . . . I don't remember."

Hallond became enraged. He stood up and leaned over the kneeling man. "You don't remember? All the wands in Gallenor have been accounted for. How is it that this child has a wand at all? If you would do your jobs, this would not be a problem! Now, think! What did it look like?!"

The soldier was now physically shaking. "I . . . I . . . don't know. He used it to cast a massive firebird spell that chased us away. I didn't have time to look closely."

"Fine, if you are unwilling to concentrate, I'll do it for you." With a sharp motion, he grabbed the soldier's forehead and began casting a powerful memory spell.

The man writhed around for a moment and tried to scream, but suddenly, he froze with a terrified look on his face. Hallond closed his eyes and focused his thoughts, searching through the man's memory. He sifted out all the useless information and came right to the moment where the man had seen the wand. It was as though Hallond was in the field, and he was looking directly through the soldier's eyes.

That very moment stood still, and Hallond saw the wand held up in the air by a young man. It was a little blurry, for the soldier was moving at the only moment he had caught a glimpse of the wand, but it was enough. Hallond abruptly let go of the soldier and stumbled backwards. The soldier fell over on the ground, muttering to himself and hardly able to do anything but shake. Hallond sat down, a shocked and displeased look written all over his face. It was the same wand he had seen in the ruby, back at the cave. It was the wand of Tolen that had carried on his mission to undermine all of Hallond's work.

"Damn you, Tolen," Hallond whispered.

Just then, two of the Tower Guards came rushing in, both stunned at the sight of the blubbering man on the ground. "What happened here?"

Hallond maintained a professional appearance and stood up. "He was attacked by a rogue wizard, and the spell has destroyed his faculties for a while. Put him in the hospital, and let the doctors take care of him." He knew full well that only another wizard could help fix this man's newfound dementia, otherwise he would spend the rest of his days as a drooling vegetable. But the Guards did not know this. They obeyed and carefully carried the soldier away from the tower.

After they left, Hallond pulled out a sheet of special paper. It was a kind created exclusively for royal orders, and only the King and his highest scribe were allowed to write on it. That, of course, mattered little to Hallond. He got a quill and ink and constructed a letter to Morris. In it, he ordered the Captain of the Royal Guard to get the boy by any means and stop him. He even gave Morris the authority to kill if necessary. Hallond was not stupid. Though he wanted the child killed, if Morris received only an order to execute a child, he would know it was not from the King and might come back questioning its origin. But right then, Hallond had little time left to handle this on his own. After he finished and used a forbidden spell to replicate the King's signature, Hallond sealed the letter with wax and pressed a royal insignia into it: an insignia he had stolen from the King.

Once he was done, he reached up and calmly pulled a string next to his desk. It rang a bell in a lower level of the tower, and sent a courier scurrying up to his room. The tower was high and his room was the tallest, so anyone coming up this far always lamented having to do so. But in moments, a spry young man arrived. He was a Lizardkind, the fastest of the races in Gallenor. Bowing low, he awaited his orders.

Hallond held out the letter. "Take this to Stillwater and make sure to hand it to Captain Morris personally. Now, go with haste." The young man bowed a little lower and then left in a hurry.

Hallond sat at his desk for a few moments, pondering all that was happening. He was so close to victory; he could not allow a simple boy to steal it from him. Surely this was nothing, and he would succeed, but the prospect of failure after a thousand years of waiting was too much to handle.

Hallond stood up and walked over to a tall stone window that looked down on the statue of the dragon in front of the walls of Thendor Castle. He had helped design the tower when the castle had been built. It was placed so that he could keep an eye on the statue at all times. The statue was the key holding back the return of the other ancients. Once the statue was destroyed and the last Dragonwand was in his possession, all his plans would fall into place. The people of Gallenor would not expect it and would wake one morning to a new life. How, then, could he allow a child the opportunity of stealing that from him? No, he would destroy this boy and the wand he carried, in spite of Tolen's foolish plans.

Captain Morris' soldier, Chris, dismounted his horse and tied her to a tree near the entrance to the forest city of the Rakki. Horses were not allowed inside these trees, so he had walked to his destination point. Morris had ordered him to confront Lord Kellus, and he would. Though, being a junior officer, he felt out of his league.

The forest was thick and crisscrossed with walkways and supports for the houses, built high above the ground. It was the duty of any officer under Morris to keep a stoic, straight face. Yet, inside these trees, Chris' awe always betrayed him. He admired the way the Rakki lived and how intricate their cities were. This city was the largest and the oldest, which showed by the amount of work that had been put into its construction.

He became lost in his admiration and had not noticed how far he had traveled into the city, or that five Rakki warriors stood in his path. The five warriors all had their bows out with arrows pointed directly at him. In front of them was the leader of the Rakki, Lord Kellus.

"Soldier of the King! What brings you back into my city?" Kellus asked directly.

Chris cleared his throat and regained the formal appearance that was expected. "Lord Kellus. I've been sent by Captain Morris of the Royal Guard to inform you that we encountered a Rakki wizard on the road."

The Rakki soldiers tightened their bowstrings in readiness to dispatch the intruder. Kellus sensed they were angry and ready to defend the life of the little girl that had just been mentioned. He held up a hand to restrain their next action. "What have you done with my citizen?"

"Your citizen fled. She evaded us with the help of another wizard boy who used a spell on the Guard."

A warm feeling of relief washed over Kellus. He trusted that Markus would protect Crystal, but now, any doubt had been removed. "I see. I'm sorry if you have been inconvenienced, but I can do nothing about the actions of one of my citizens who has left the boundaries of my domain."

"Captain Morris has sent me with a warning. Aiding and abetting criminals is a high crime in Gallenor, one that even your position cannot protect you from. After he apprehends the girl, a full investigation will be enacted here."

"I see. If that happens, I will cooperate as far as the law requires. Until then, please do not return, making threats in my trees. It disturbs the peace."

Chris huffed and turned to leave.

"Did you see her?" Kellus asked.

"What?"

"Did you see the girl wizard?" Kellus was smiling and waiting for the young soldier to answer.

Chris turned around with a furrowed brow. "Yes. Why?"

"How old was she?"

"I don't know. Fourteen. If you think acting dumb about her identity now will—"

"She's sixteen. Just turned sixteen a few days ago. The young man with her is the same age, perhaps even a little younger."

Chris realized what Kellus had just said. "So, you *do* know who we're talking about! You were aware of her and hid her from the Guard." He pulled out his blade. "By order of the—"

With a sharp ping, an arrow hit the blade perfectly, and sent it flying out of Chris' hand. Then another stuck the ground right beside his foot to demonstrate how close he was to being dispatched himself.

"Wait!" Kellus stopped his warriors. "Do not kill him." He stepped forward toward Chris.

"What are you doing? Are you going to imprison me?" Chris asked.

"No." Kellus shook his head. "I asked you those questions to help you understand the dangers here. The boy and girl you encountered are children. They have never harmed anyone. In fact, the boy saved the life of one of my own when an imp attacked. Can you accept what you are doing? Can the morals in your heart justify taking those children and putting them in a prison? How about the mother and father of the girl? They have been locked away for four long years, while she has cried in her sleep for them. What good has this accomplished?"

For the first time, Chris felt a hint of sorrow in his heart for what they had done. "It . . . we . . . we are only following orders. It is for the best for all of Gallenor."

"Do you truly believe that? Can you acknowledge you are the reason that girl has cried herself to sleep each night? Can you live with the hundreds of other children deprived of their parents, brothers, sisters, and grandparents you have stolen from them? Has anyone ever truly provided you with a good enough reason to sate such guilt that should be filling your soul?"

Chris picked up his sword and slowly sheathed it. He wanted to find the right answer, but there wasn't one. "I . . . I don't know."

"You don't know what?"

"I just . . . don't know. I . . . I have to go." Chris turned and left, his emotions in turmoil as he sorted between his own convictions and loyalty to the crown.

The five warriors kept a keen eye on Chris until he was past their trees. Finally, they lowered their weapons and backed down. The chief among them asked Kellus, "What now?"

"Now, my friend, we hope that young man has a change of heart."

The woman to his right said, "That's a lot to hope for. What if they send the legion here?"

"I trust in hope, but I am not foolish. Call in all the scouts and imp hunters. We will strengthen our own borders and wait for news from Treb and Kiin."

"Aye, sir." The Commander and his best warriors moved out quickly to fulfill his orders.

Kellus was a clever man. Not only was he securing their borders by calling back all their best hunters, he was leaving the blue forests undefended. The imps wouldn't be kept at bay any longer. If the legion did come in to attack the Rakki, they would encounter the imp infestation in the forest before they even made it to the border of the city. It was their own fault. The Royal Guard had been in charge of imp patrols for years, before the wizard hunts began. The Rakki were doing the Crown a favor by picking up the slack. Now, it would be the problem of the Royal Guard again.

"All right, you two, stay with Treb. I'll go see if my old friend is still here." Kiin walked away from her three companions. Years ago, she had come to Stillwater as Kellus' personal security, during a trade negotiation between their village and Stillwater.

Crystal quietly asked her father, "Where's Mother going?"

"She's going to ask an old friend for some information," he quietly responded.

Markus frowned. "Why don't we just ask a friendly vendor or farmer? I'm sure they won't mind speaking to us."

"We need to know what the Royal Guard is doing and how they patrol up and down the barren roads northward of here. If we ask the wrong person such questions, it's likely to get us caught by the Guard before we can get out of here. Right now, we just need to look for supplies and try not to look too conspicuous."

They walked down the vendor road and noticed a lot of the stalls were packing up for the evening. "Drat, we're too late," Markus grumped.

"Are you looking for anything special?" Donna interrupted them, having come around her booth to greet the handsome new traveler.

Treb turned and noticed her grinning at him. "Uh, well, we're looking for traveling supplies, a mat, some food, that kind of stuff. Do you sell anything like that?"

Donna pouted. "No, I'm the local apothecary. But," she brightened right back up, "it wouldn't be wise to go on a long trip without getting some of the best medical potions around. And I'll sell them to you at a very fine price."

Treb rubbed his chin. They could use some medicine for the road. He always traveled with at least a bottle of stomach aid potion, and with the two kids, it might be a good idea to stock up. "Show me what you have."

She led him over to her booth and started unpacking everything. "The very best for all occasions. Take a look. I'll give you anything you want for half price."

"That's very generous." He started picking up bottles and looking at the liquids.

She leaned over, shamelessly pushing her chest out a little. "So, who was that?" she pointed in the general direction of where Kiin had walked.

Treb, not paying attention, thought she was pointing at Crystal. "Oh, that's my daughter."

"Oh, my. You don't look old enough to have a daughter that age." She was certainly surprised.

He held a bottle up and looked through the liquid. "Oh, she isn't my real daughter; she's adopted. But, I love her like she's my own."

Donna smiled and looked up and down his bare, furry, well-defined chest. "Oh, that's so sweet. You're a very handsome man."

"Huh?" He hadn't quite caught what she had said.

She corrected herself. *"Responsible,* responsible man."

"Oh." He frowned at her, not sure what to make of the way she was ruthlessly flirting with him.

"Hey, Dad, what're you looking at?" Crystal approached with Markus right behind her.

He looked through another liquid again. "These are potions—stomach aids we might need on the road."

Donna grinned at the Rakki girl and the human boy. "The very best potions in Gallenor, I assure you." She was amused at the two of them. Could this man be so generous with his time and attention that he would adopt three children, and one not even being a member of his race? Some women might find that a turn off, but it only turned her on more.

"Are these stomach aid potions good for all races' stomachs? We have—"

"Oh, yes. My potions will work for anyone. Rakki, human, even Shlan." She was an eager salesperson.

Markus looked at some of the potions, as did Crystal. He calmly stated, "I wanted to learn some potion blending if I'd gotten to go to the wizardry college. I hope I can find someone to teach me once we free the wizards. OW!" Crystal had stepped on his foot.

She whispered through clenched teeth, "Don't talk about

wizards!"

Donna could not help but overhear his words, yet chose to not ask him about wizards for the time being. She smiled at Markus and looked at the potion he was examining. "Do you like that? It's a potion to turn your hair red. I find it works better than some of the treatments at the beauty shops."

Markus smiled back at her and returned the bottle to the booth. "No, I don't think I would like red hair."

She turned to Crystal. "I'd love to see how it worked on a species with fur all over. Would you like to try it out and let me know the results? I assure you, it won't do you any harm. A gift." She held the bottle up to Crystal.

Crystal smiled but shook her head. "No, thank you. Perhaps another time."

Kiin came back from looking for her friend and did not look pleased. "I couldn't find Mary. Someone told me they thought she moved to Maliden Port a few months ago."

Treb smiled at Donna and then handed her a handful of coins. "Thanks." He put the bottles in the pack Markus carried and then walked everyone away from the booth. "We'll just have to be careful. I suggest we get out of town as soon as possible and find somewhere we can camp away from the guards."

"Daddy!" Crystal grabbed his arm and pointed down the street. She hid behind him while still holding his arm. He looked up to see there was a Royal Guard walking their way with a torch in his hands. The sun was setting, but it was not time for torches yet. This meant the Guard was going to be patrolling for the evening.

Treb let out a sigh. "It'll be hard getting out of this city."

Kiin began walking toward another street, directing everyone to follow her so they would not happen upon the Guard by accident. "I don't see how we can get out without being stopped for questioning. After dusk, they always check people coming and going from a walled city like this. We'll have to stay somewhere."

"We can't. What if they come in the night to inspect the rooms? I'd rather be away from anyone who might be looking for us," Treb whispered to his wife and then noticed another Guard coming up another street.

Markus spoke up, "Whatever we do, we'd better do it quickly."

"Hey, you! Stop!" A Guard surprised them as he came around a corner and approached quickly.

Treb held Crystal's hand and sort of put her behind him. "What is it, sir?"

The slightly portly, middle-aged Guard glared at them. "I'm sure you're new here, but Stillwater has a curfew for all children under the age of eighteen. They must be inside, or we'll have to cite you."

Treb calmly nodded. "We're new. Thank you for telling us. Where can we find lodging?"

"Come with me, I'll show you to the Waterwell Inn. Hey, wait . . ." he looked down into his pocket and there was a red glow. To everyone's dismay, he pulled out a sensing stone that was glowing bright red. "What is this? You . . . you're a wizard." He was shocked. It had been some time since they had found a wizard roaming the streets of Stillwater.

Treb was growling and glaring at the shorter man. "You'll leave us alone, or I will—"

Suddenly, the Guard dropped his torch and the stone and pulled out his sword. "No threats, wizards, or I will have to do something drastic."

Crystal was about to suggest that Markus do something, like use the same firebird spell again, when a woman's hand ran down the shoulder of the Guard and gently pulled him to the side.

Donna stood there and rubbed a potion against his armor. The vapors entered his nose, and he became a little dazed.

She smiled at him and watched as the light amnesia potion erased a bit of his short-term memory. "I'm so sorry to have stumbled into you. You had better go get it before it gets away."

He looked at his sword and then at her. "Huh, what am I doing?"

She pretended to be terribly surprised. "Didn't you hear? A woman screamed that an imp was seen flying around the flower district. Go, before it does something bad." She pointed off to the furthest part of the city.

The Guard looked around and then ran off, certain he was supposed to stop an imp attack within the city walls.

Donna watched him leave. Once he was out of view, she looked back to Treb. "Come, you can stay with me."

Kiin frowned and was more than confused. "Who are you?"

Donna smiled and then looked down at the burning torch against the ground, a fire hazard, for sure. She held out her hand, saying, "Vatn." A small mist formed in the air around her hand, then it congealed into a large blob of water with which she proceeded to douse the flames. "A fellow wizard who refuses to be taken into captivity. Now, unless you want another encounter with a Guard, I suggest you get into my shop." She hurried them along. "Oh, and this." Reaching down, she picked up the sensing stone. "I hate these things." With a quick toss, she sent the stone flying over the city wall and into the forest on the other side.

Treb and Kiin looked at each other. This was highly unusual, but it was an opportunity they would not pass up. They followed the kids into the potion shop.

CHAPTER 12: DONNA

DONNA walked them to the back of the shop and picked up a fake potion bottle, causing the small pedestal of wood, under the bottle, to lift. This activated a series of levers and doors that moved the shelf of potions to the side and revealed a secret entrance to a basement. Without any words between them, they followed Donna down the stairs.

Before she had gotten halfway down, she turned to see that they were all inside the small stairwell. With a clever smile and a pull on a torch holder on the wall, the torch lit up with a sudden burst of flames, and the secret entrance sealed itself behind them. From there, she continued down the short walk to a dirt floor basement.

"Eldr." Donna pointed a finger at the wall, and a small flame shot out, igniting another torch. Donna repeated this action several more times, lighting up the room for them. The last spell she used was the same as the others, only bigger, and it ignited the fireplace.

Treb, Kiin, Crystal, and Markus cautiously walked in and found places to sit. Donna prepared a pot of water over the fire. She used a spigot on the wall that was probably fed by the river right outside the building.

"So, what are wizards doing in Stillwater?" she asked without real concern in her voice.

Treb cleared his throat and answered, "What gave you the impression we were wizards?"

Donna stopped and gave him a half-cocked smirk. "First, that sensing stone caught on quickly. Second, when you were at my stand, those two were talking about magic and wizardry."

Kiin shot Crystal and Markus a serious glare. "They should've known better than to give themselves away."

Donna poured the last pail of water into the pot over the fire. "So, is it just the young children, or are you two wizards as well?"

Crystal looked as though she were going to answer, but was stopped by her father. Treb asked, "Why should we trust you with such incriminating information?"

"Look, I just saved your butts from the Guards. I think that earns a little trust."

Treb agreed with her to a point. "For that, we're thankful. But my daughter's life is at stake if anyone finds out she is a wizard. I cannot go around trusting everyone, especially people we've just met."

Donna stood up and walked over to a cabinet filled with vials of potions. "True, so, introductions are in order. My name is Donna. I'm a potion master and wizard. Four years ago, I escaped the

Guards' notice by hiding in this very basement, waiting for them to escort all the wizards out of Stillwater."

Crystal asked, "Didn't they know you were a wizard? Surely, being a local potion wizard would be known."

Donna smiled at the pretty little girl as she picked out a phial among the many. "Not really. When the decree was issued, I was very new to Stillwater. No one here knew I was a wizard. They all thought I was just a potion maker. So no one turned me in. Also, to be honest, I'm not very powerful at basic magic. Those sensing stones don't go off as quickly around me."

Markus asked, "Over the past four years, you've not been turned in once?"

"Dozens of times. I've been inspected by every sensing stone in this city. Every time there's a general inspection, I'm one of the first to be questioned. I know they'll never fully believe me, but nothing they use can convict me, so I'm free. A few locals are aware of the truth, but they're trusted friends who would not turn on me. In fact, I have a girl who helps out in the shop. She's an apprentice potion maker, not a wizard, but a smart girl. She's fully aware of the truth, and I would trust her with my life if it came to that." With a great motherly smile, she walked over to the pot. "I bet you guys would like a nice chicken stew."

Kiin nodded. "Oh, yes. We haven't had any good chicken in a

few days now."

Donna poured the potion into the water and then began to stir it around. The magical blend of herbs, spices, and other various items began to transform the mundane liquid into a heavy soup filled with vegetables and chicken meat. "So, when I realized they would come around often, checking for wizards, I knew I had to come up with something to disguise myself. I created a special potion. When I rub it on, it fools their sensing stones and mirrors. Unfortunately, I think it only works on me because I'm not powerful as a wizard."

Markus chimed in. "But a clever one."

Donna turned and gave him a big smile. "Oh, thanks. Now, you know all about me. What about yourselves? Are you running from being found, or are you looking for something?"

Treb looked at his wife and then at Markus. He felt it was not right to tell her about the Dragonwand and their quest. "Uh, we're just travelers. Kiin and I aren't wizards, but Markus and Crystal are."

"I understand. It was when I heard the King ordered even children to be taken from their homes and families that I knew this was not right. There was something horribly wrong with this law. I fear their promises to release wizards, when they find that Dragonwand, is just a hoax. They'll keep the wizards under lock and key because of some unfounded paranoia."

Crystal looked down. "That's my biggest fear. I don't know if I'll ever see my real parents again."

Donna snapped her fingers, and the wooden spoon continued stirring the stew on its own. She turned to look at Crystal. "Oh, my. They took both of your parents?"

Crystal nodded.

"Oh, my dear child, how terrible. What of you, boy? Did they take your parents as well?" Donna looked over to Markus.

Markus shook his head. He had a hard time saying the truth, knowing how hard it might be on Crystal. "No. Only my father had any magical abilities, and he left those behind a long time ago. I doubt even the sensing stones could detect it in him. I never thought I would be thankful to say that, but at least I know they're safe."

Donna wanted to ask why the boy was with the group if his parents were okay. But she felt she had pried enough. "Okay, who wants some dinner?" she happily announced and grabbed a set of wooden bowls from a shelf near her.

"Oh, that does smell good." Treb sniffed the air. All the Rakki in the room were lifting their faces up and sniffing the glorious scent in the air.

Donna happily served out four bowls of her famous instant chicken stew, one of her best sellers back when she wasn't afraid of showing off a few of her magical potions. Simple potion blenders without magic could not create such things, so she didn't usually make the dish for anyone but herself. "Eat up. That vial of potion makes a big kettle of soup."

Treb ate a big spoonful, but then sort of looked bored with it.

Donna walked over to him with a worried look in her eyes. "Oh, is it not good?" Of all of them, she wanted him to like her stew.

Treb faked a smile and shook his head. "Oh, it's fine. Just fine," he lied.

Donna was not so easily deceived. "If it isn't good, I can make something else. Those instant stews are not hard to make. What's wrong with it? Too old, bitter, sour, what?"

Treb was about to be gallant again, but Markus piped up. "I don't think it's bad; just not spicy enough for their tastes."

"Oh, how silly of me. I forgot. You're Rakki. Wait." She ran off in a big hurry and went into another room of the basement.

Markus was eagerly eating up the delicious stew, enjoying every bite. Crystal looked over to him with a frown. "How can you eat that? It has no taste."

Markus wiped his mouth on his sleeve and laughed. "Not to you, but to me, it's fine."

Donna came back in with another vial of something. It was a

translucent golden liquid. "Here, this'll help." She went to Treb first and took out the tiny cork. With a tip up, she dripped a few drops into his stew and then stirred it around for him with his spoon. Crystal could see Donna was a little too close and showing a bit too much of her bust to Treb as she did this. Kiin wasn't jealous; it was more a matter of confusion.

Donna looked into his eyes and amorously said, "There, taste it now."

Treb kindly took another bite and his eyes lit up. "Oh, this is perfect. Just the right thing: spice."

Kiin held out her bowl. "Sounds perfect." Donna added some to Kiin's and then headed over to Crystal, not stopping to stir theirs as she had the handsome Treb's.

When she got to Markus, he pulled his back. "Uh, no thank you. I'm not as keen on spice as these guys. What's that? A special seasoning potion?

Donna replaced the cork and shook her head. "Nope, just one of the many ingredients I use in making other potions. This is pure mountain vine pepper oil."

Markus coughed at the thought. "Vine pepper oil! That's the hottest stuff in Gallenor."

Crystal grinned at him as she swallowed a mouthful of the now hot-as-fire stew. "Perfect."

Markus shuddered. "I don't think I'll ever get used to that."

The evening passed quietly, as they had their dinner. Then Donna placed some mats on the floor of the basement for the kids. For some reason, she placed three, but took care to put them near enough the fireplace so they would all be good and warm. Treb was offered a guest bed she had in another room.

While they got their beds ready, Donna went back up and brought in the rest of her stock from the booth. To get just half of her stuff inside was not only bad if a thief happened by, but it might raise suspicion, and that was the last thing they needed right now.

Markus and Crystal sat on a bench in the basement, watching the fire. Treb kept a close eye on them as they sat together, but Kiin was keeping an eye on Treb.

Watching Treb and Kiin leave the room, Markus waited until they were out of earshot to ask Crystal something. "Hey, you okay?"

"What do you mean?"

"You've been a little upset the last few hours. I know you can be shy, but you look angry. Did I do something wrong?"

"No, it's not you. It's me."

"You?"

"Yeah, it's me." Crystal shook her head in disgust. "I can't believe I acted so childish earlier."

Markus thought hard about what she had just said. He couldn't pinpoint what "earlier" she was talking about. "When did this happen?"

"You know, when we stopped running from that scary Guard and I broke down and went all to pieces. I . . . I acted just like I did when I was twelve and my parents were first taken from me. I acted like a baby!" She was angry at herself.

Markus smiled at her and took her hand. "No, you acted scared. It's okay to be scared. That man took your parents from you, which can only bring back terrible memories. I can't imagine what it felt like to come face to face with him again."

"For four years, I've had the same nightmare: that terrible man coming into my room and taking me away. He puts me where I cannot find anyone I love, and everyone who loves me is lost, looking for me far, far away."

He rubbed his thumb over her hand gently, brushing it across the fur. "I don't know what it's like to walk right into the nightmare of my life. I don't know what I would do. I would probably act just like you did, scared and panicking. But I wouldn't be mad at myself for it. It's hard to face your fear like that."

She growled a little, which was extremely cute, and glared at nothing in particular. Though, in her mind, she could see that awful human soldier who had torn her family apart. "Next time, I'll face my fear. I won't go crying to my father. I'll set Captain Morris' furless hide on fire and force him to feel the pain I've felt all these years."

Markus did his best not to laugh. The sight of her showing strength was cute and surprisingly attractive. "I'll be there with you. We'll find the wand and do what we have to, so those responsible can be brought to justice."

She stopped looking so angry and kind of leaned her head over to him. "You know, there was something I treasured from that experience."

"What?"

Crystal looked up at him with soft eyes. "The way you told me you would protect me. That you wouldn't let them take me away." Her eyes were looking directly into his. "I wanted to thank you."

He smiled, a little embarrassed. "Oh, it was nothing. Really. I, uh . . . what are you doing?" He noticed she was getting closer to him.

"Thanking you." She surprised him with a kiss—his first. For a few moments, they kissed an awkward teenager kiss, but it was fantastic for both of them.

In the doorway to the dark room adjacent to them, there was a pair of glinting eyes and a deep growling. Treb's fists were clenched, and he was baring all of his fangs. If it were not for a kind hand pushing him back, he might have done something terrible to Markus right then.

"Honey, get ahold of yourself. It's just a kiss." Kiin stopped him.

He whispered through his fangs, "But . . . but, she and he . . . they are . . ."

"Just kissing. She's sixteen. It's about time she kissed her first boy. The world won't end if you don't blow up." Kiin was always able to keep Treb at bay, no matter how furious he was.

Treb's eyes were glued on the kissing kids. "If he touches any part of her, I will . . ."

"Look, honey, they stopped. It was only a kiss. Now cool off. You're going to grind your teeth off if you keep gritting them like that." She found it hilarious.

Markus sat beside Crystal, a dazed expression on his face. Crystal was grinning like a fool, and horribly embarrassed. She didn't know that anyone had watched, but it didn't keep her from feeling self-conscious. What had she just done? She had never thought she would do something like that, but it was like there had been only one option.

"Crystal, that was . . . *amazing*!" Markus had liked it—a lot.

She blushed under her fur. "I was just so thankful, and, well, I kind of, you know . . . uh . . . like you."

Markus wanted to jump around for joy at her saying so, but his testosterone prevented him from doing so. "The feeling, I guess, you know, it's the same . . . from me."

"So, what are you two doing?" Kiin came in at that moment, having decided they had had enough time to recover from their experience.

Crystal almost fell off of the bench as Markus jumped to his feet and was about ten yards away from her in two seconds. "Uh, we weren't doing anything," he said.

Crystal added, "Yeah, Markus was just . . . asking me about . . . something."

Kiin did her best not to laugh at them. "Asking about what?" she egged them on.

Markus tried to think of a good answer. "Oh, uh, yeah, something . . ." Then he had an idea. There was actually something he *did* want to ask her. "Could you show me more about healing magic? I think it'd be smart if we both could use those spells of yours. When I healed that arrow wound, it was kind of neat. Yeah, that's something."

Crystal sat up straight and tried to look normal. "Uh, sure, yeah, I can teach you all that I know."

Kiin straightened out the mats again and sat down on the middle mat so that she would be between the kids for the night. "Why don't you two talk about that in the morning? It's bed time."

Happy, embarrassed, thrilled, and a little confused, Crystal and Markus lay down on the floor in front of the fireplace. Treb had suggested, only moments ago, that Markus could move his mat into the room where Treb slept to separate the kids with a stone wall. But Kiin explained to him that a warm fire was nicer than a cold floor, and to stop worrying so much. She would stay with them for the night, and everything would be all right. This didn't sate his fears, but he hardly won arguments with her and knew when to give up.

Treb stood in the corner of the room he had been given. The room was not entirely enclosed. In fact, there were two large doorways at the far end without doors hanging in them. One doorway led into the basement den where the others slept for the night. The other door opened into a dark set of rooms where Donna kept her potion making ingredients. It also led to the stairwell back up to her shop.

Right then, Treb was taking off his armor and washing his face in a bowl of water Donna had brought him earlier. For a moment, he contemplated taking off his pants to sleep, as he did at home, in his undergarments. Little did he know, his back was being watched by a set of pleased eyes. He soaked a washcloth with some of the water and ran it up and down his upper arms where the armor tied on. He got particularly sweaty there.

Without warning, a soft hand ran down his tail. Over and over, gently and with good motion, the hand softly stroked his tail, which was a pleasing sensation for any Rakki. Treb smiled, as he was always happy to let Kiin pet his fur. Then another hand ran down his bare back, feeling his furry muscles, which tickled but only made him smile all the more. He was surprised Kiin would be so amorous right now, but he wasn't going to stop her yet.

"My, you have lovely fur." Donna's voice shocked the romance right out of him.

Treb was so startled, he jerked forward and smacked right into the wall, knocking the wooden bowl of water to the floor. He turned around, holding his face with one hand where he had met stone wall, his other hand holding his tail—keeping it close to him and away from her. "Donna! What are you doing?" He attempted to contain his yelling, so as not to wake anyone, especially Kiin.

Donna gave him a very sultry smile and was sort of pushing her chest at him. "Oh, I just thought such a handsome, virile man like you needed a good woman."

"Donna, what . . . I . . . how . . ." He was stammering and still holding his tail against him.

She pressed him up against the wall, her body leaning against his. Looking at his lips, she bit her bottom lip and grinned. Then her eyes turned up to look into his. "How fortunate I've found a man who is not afraid of having a family, but you should really consider adding a mother to this brood of children."

"Mother?!"

Donna grabbed him by the arms and pulled him in closer. "Yes, a woman who can teach your children about magic and life, and who can make your life much more exciting." She forcibly laid her head on his chest, put her arms around him, and used her hands to get a nice firm grip on his butt. "Whatever you need, I can provide it to you. Let's make sweet music, my hunk of furry muscle."

Treb was just about to lose his fur at that moment, because he was so shocked. "But . . . I already have a wife!"

Donna stepped back with her mouth agape. "A wife! You're married?!"

"Of course I'm married! Who do you think Kiin is!?" Treb was angry, and still shocked.

Donna backed up. "But . . . but, you said that she was your daughter?"

Just then, Kiin came into the room with her bow and an arrow out. She looked around for what enemy had caused Treb to yell. "Honey, what is it?"

Treb smiled at her and endeavored to appear less shocked. He wasn't sure if she would get angry at this situation, so it was best to not tell her about it. "Go back to bed. It was nothing. Donna just startled me."

Kiin looked around to make sure everything was okay, then she smiled at her husband and left the room.

Donna sat on the bed, highly disappointed and embarrassed. "Oh, I'm so sorry, Mr. Treb. I would never have . . . what an idiot. I'm so sorry."

Treb gathered himself and finally let go of his tail so he could not appear so frightened. "It's all right, just a simple misunderstanding."

"Okay, so, Kiin is your wife, and Crystal and Markus are your children?"

"Not quite. Crystal is my adopted daughter, but Markus is just a friend and traveling companion. And Kiin is my wife." He wanted to repeat that last statement.

Donna got up and headed out. "I'm just so sorry. I . . . I'll leave you to get some sleep. I'm sorry."

Treb sat on the bed and let out a tightly held sigh. This was certainly not what he had been expecting tonight.

CHAPTER 13: WIZARDS AMONG US

THE Royal Guard office was quiet this time of night, but then again, with a curfew and so many Guards around the city, it was always quiet at this hour. The local constabulary branch of the Guard was out patrolling the city. The Blue Forests may have had a bad imp problem, but with the amount showing up from the Barren Mountains, the city could become infested quickly. So the Guards spent each night, making sure to watch for imps and keep them from disturbing the life of the citizens of Stillwater.

Captain Morris couldn't care less about imps or about the menial security matters of Stillwater. In four years, he had not been so easily evaded by a wizard. Then again, most came willingly, obedient to the Royal decree. The few that did flee were often caught within hours. But the Rakki and the human seemed to have great skill in evasion. He anticipated that along the road to Stillwater, he would find them, but that had not happened. Then, he had expected that once he got to the city, the local legion of Royal Guard would already have had them in custody. But that was not the case either. Now, there were no signs of them anywhere, and it was making him mad. The few officers here were reluctant to speak with him at all, considering how he was fuming today.

Morris had planned on leaving the city and simply informing the local Royal Guard of the rogue wizards. But then came the Royal Courier with a strange message meant for Morris only. The wizard boy he had seen was now a priority objective. Only once since the original ordering of the decree four years ago, had any single wizard been a priority objective: Tolen. Did the King believe this child knew something about Tolen's dealings? How dangerous could an untrained wizard kid be? In his twenty years of service to the crown, Morris had never questioned an order from the King. If it had come from any other ranking official, Morris would have returned to Thendor to get all the details. But this order bore the stamp and signature of the King, thus Morris readied himself to find the child at any cost.

"Sir?" An older Commander of the station approached the desk where Morris pored over incident reports from the constabulary.

Morris did not even look up when he barked, "What!"

"Uh, you've been reading those reports for six hours, and it's far past midnight. Surely you need to get some rest." He was being a good subordinate to think of his superior's welfare.

Morris did not see it that way, though. "I will tell you when I need rest."

"Understood." The Commander also knew when to not push a superior officer. He turned sharply to leave.

"Wait. Come back," Morris ordered the older soldier. "I need you to ready all the men you can spare, tomorrow morning. We are going to canvas the city first thing."

The Commander frowned. "Canvas . . . Stillwater. For what? We have the imp situation under control."

"I'm not looking for imps. I'm looking for wizards." Morris glanced over to the Royal Decree he had received.

"Wizards? But, we have that under control. Each of my men carries a sensing stone and are told to take into custody any wizard found."

"I'm not questioning your men's actions." Morris pinched the space between his eyes. "They're a credit to the Kingdom, I'm sure. But there's a priority wizard on the loose, and I believe he might be here in Stillwater."

"Priority? The Wizard Tolen?" Every Guard knew that name.

"No. Tolen is dead. I witnessed his death myself." He glanced over at the Royal Decree. "There's another. A child seems to have worried the King."

"A child, sir?" This was highly unusual. The idea of making a child a priority objective to the Guard was unheard of.

Morris glared at the Commander. "Yes, a child. I suspect he might know something about the Dragonwand we've been searching for. He might even have something to do with Tolen's plans. Either way, it doesn't matter to you. The King has made his order clear to me, and I'll see to it that it is followed to the letter. If you have a problem with that, I can relieve you of your duties and find another commander who'll be willing to follow the King's orders."

The Commander stood at attention. "I will do as you ask. My men are at your command."

"Good. When dawn breaks tomorrow, have them come here, and we'll begin the search. Lock down the city tonight and don't let anyone leave. Send patrols out on the roads, starting as soon as possible, and make sure anyone who is found is inspected thoroughly. I'll not allow a runner on my watch."

"Yes, sir. At once." The Commander had all sorts of questions about such orders, but he knew better than to voice them now. Out the door he went, with the haste of a Shlan, to make sure Captain Morris' orders were fulfilled quickly.

Morris sat down at the desk and looked over the orders again. Something about them struck him, for they specifically mentioned the wand the child carried. When they brought in the boy, the wand was to be accounted for and kept under guard until it was brought before the King and Hallond. It made Morris wonder if this child had somehow found the Dragonwand, which would end their four-year-long search.

After stacking up all the important documents so he could keep them to himself, Morris left the office to go and get some rest.

Markus stood out on a hill near Stillwater. He was alone in the dark of night. He could not remember going out there, or why he was alone. Suddenly, a great roar echoed in the distance. He saw a dragon flying with flame-drenched wings, outstretched. It was searching for something, because its head was darting around, scanning the ground. Markus highly feared this dragon. He knew this dragon, and it was extremely bad news. But he had no idea why.

"Oh, no, not again!" He realized it was one of his bad dreams, the first in many nights now.

"Tolen! Where are you!?" the dragon yelled out in a deep, desperate voice. Then its eyes fell upon Markus, who was standing on the hill. "Where are you?! I must find you!

Markus turned to run, but he could no more outrun a dragon than he could fly. He stopped running and realized something. "This is my dream. I will not let it win. Wand!" he called out, and a new wand appeared in his hand. It was not a small magic wand, but a staff. Markus knew this staff. He trusted it and was ready to use it to fight the dragon.

The dragon raced toward Markus, its eyes fixed on the wand.

"Give it to me! Tolen will not stop me!"

"ELDR!" Markus yelled, and a huge torrent of flame shot out and blasted the dragon. It did nothing.

"I will destroy every last part of you, Tolen! Even this child!"

Just as the dragon got to Markus, another dragon appeared and rammed it out of the sky. The new dragon was white with golden highlights covering him. It lurched back, releasing a volley of lightning at the other dragon, and sent it even farther away.

Markus was about to ask its name, or who the other dragon was, when it suddenly turned on him and commanded, "WAKE!"

Markus sat up on his mat with the last word of the strange dream echoing in his ears. He half expected to hear the booming sounds of a thunderstorm outside, but the night was clear. After a moment or two, he lied down and tried to go back to sleep. The dream did not disturb him, as it might others, for he had dreamt of strange things for so long. The only element that struck him as odd was that the evil dragon had seemed to be searching for him, even though it had stared right at him. Markus simply shook it off and turned over to go back to sleep. His dreams for the rest of the night were not as frightening.

Hallond fell back from where he had been holding tightly to a large mirror in his tower. The surface was rippling like water with blue electricity dancing across it.

Suddenly, he held a hand to his head. It felt like ice had just filled his brain. "GAH! Dammit!" It was always painful for a wizard to be forced out of a spell right in the middle of its casting. The pain would subside, but the rage wasn't going to fade as quickly. With a terse slicing motion of his hand in the air, he canceled the magic, and the mirror returned to its normal, placid appearance.

Hallond slowly rose from the floor and closed the windows. The spell had made the room hot while it was cast. Now it was over, and the chilly night air quickly cooled down his old body. All the while, he muttered to himself, "So, Tolen, you found a boy willing to fight for you. He's brave, I'll give him that." He paused before closing the last window. "And here I thought fighting a child would be easy. It might prove a little more difficult if he is this brash. Then again, his bravery might just be his undoing."

With a quick slam, he closed the last window and left his tower to get some rest. His aged body was easily tired, and he had a lot of work to do.

Fredrick, the head of Stillwater's City Guard, came in early that morning. He had prepared everything to Morris' specifications and was happy to tell this to the illustrious Captain. Morris, who had come in with a sour mood, had been barking at everyone. Perhaps Morris would look favorably on Fredrick for his diligence.

But when he came into his office, he found Captain Morris was not there yet. Then he discovered that Morris had already come and gone. There was a letter on the desk with Fredrick's name on it. He opened it and read the part where Morris was demoting him and placing the next in line in command of Stillwater. His reasons: he didn't like Fredrick.

Fredrick was furious. He had been a loyal servant of Gallenor for years and worked very hard to earn his position. Now, Morris was stripping him of his rank simply because he didn't like him? It wasn't just rude; it was unprofessional. Morris had some nerve. He might have been the Captain of all the Guard of Gallenor, but he had a responsibility to be a great leader, not a tyrant.

It was then that Fredrick noticed something odd on the table. There sat a royal letter; the paper was unmistakable. Few royal letters came here. What was normally received were the copies written on the less important paper. This was truly a unique occurrence. Perhaps this would explain Morris' unusual behavior.

Fredrick opened it and began to read. It was the letter from the King to Morris about making a boy a priority objective. This struck Fredrick as unusual. Why would a boy be so dangerous? What could possibly make this seem logical? Well, that was between the King and Morris. Fredrick should have left it alone, but something about it didn't seem right.

Fredrick Greystone was probably the oldest serving soldier in Stillwater, even older than Morris. He had been serving for decades and was loyal to his mission. He had seen a few of these letters in his time, and he knew something seemed peculiar about this one in particular. Its handwriting was a bit off, and the wording was not normal for a royal decree issued by King Anthony. Maybe the King's age had changed his style, or maybe this was a fraud. Perhaps Fredrick should bring this up with Morris? Or, perhaps he should send it back to Thendor to let the palace have a look. If they didn't see anything wrong, then nothing would happen. But, if they discovered a strange conspiracy, then Morris would be in trouble for not investigating this himself. Somehow, that notion made the old Guard smile.

With a careful wrapping of the letter, and a quick visit to the hawk keeper, the letter was sent on its way back to the palace. After that, Fredrick would play dumb if Morris wondered what had happened to his letter. The sun was coming up, and the canvasing of Stillwater was about to begin. There was a decidedly sneaky smile on Fredrick's face as he readied himself to leave.

A master blacksmith slammed his hammer down on the anvil to

shape a hunk of metal in the early stages of becoming the needed parts for the carriage maker. Each hit was loud and echoed throughout his forge. Once he was satisfied with how much he had altered it, he thrust the metal into a bucket of water to cool off.

Setting the hammer down, he pulled out a cloth to wipe sweat from his brow. "All right, the first thing you must remember is to keep your water full and near you. That metal is blazing hot and could easily set something on fire if you make a mistake." He spoke to a group of young children.

This time of the year, the children who had turned fifteen began to seek their future job, if they hadn't already chosen. Not everyone in the room would become a blacksmith, but they would learn about the process, helping them make their decision.

A boy spoke up. "Master William, can you show us how to make a sword?"

"Sorry, Jonathan, but I don't make swords. I know how, but I don't have what I need. The blacksmiths who make swords are in Thendor and Mildrani City." He wiped his forehead again and picked up the hammer. "All right. I'll show you the proper way to swing this hammer and how to do so without hurting your arm." He swung it over his head and then let it clang against the anvil. "Let it bounce; don't hold it tight, or you'll injure you wrist and elbow— and it doesn't go well for the smithing work, either." He did it again and hit even harder. Each time, the forge echoed with a rather loud clang and bang at the same time. "Sometimes, you have to let it . . . do you hear something?"

There was a loud banging on the door. Then, without giving him a chance to answer it, someone kicked the door in. A mixed group of City and Royal Guards spilled down the steps into his forge.

Master William was not amused. "Look here, I'm in the middle of a class. This forge is off limits to anyone, even the Guard, without permission. It's for your own safety."

While the City Guard sort of backed up, the Royal Guard marched down the steps and came up to William. The Commander scoffed, "Nothing is off limits to Royal Guard."

"What do you want?" William set his hammer down so as not to look threatening.

The Guards all pulled out sensing stones and began to walk around the room. The Commander held up a paper signed by the new Captain of the City Guard. "We're looking for wizards. Your cooperation is appreciated." His tone was dry and uncaring.

William was appalled. "These are just children, and I certainly have passed enough of your tests. There are no adults in this room." Just then, one of the Guards grabbed an older boy by his collar and lifted him up. The sensing stone had reflected the glow of the furnace for a moment, but upon closer inspection, it did not show a true glow. The Royal Guard carelessly dropped the child.

William was furious. He even took hold of his hammer. "Now, see here!"

The Commander slapped the paper onto William's chest and then let it fall to the ground. "Thank you for your time. Have a nice day."

The frightening invasion of the class's lesson was over when the Guards left through the door they had destroyed. A young girl picked up the paper and read it. "Master William, they're searching for a child wizard."

William took the paper from her to read it himself. "A child . . . they're taking children now? What's this world coming to?" He tossed the paper into the fire. "Sorry you had to see that, children. Please remain calm, and let's continue with the demonstration. Oh, Reha, could you go and prop the door back up? I don't want any more interruptions."

"Yes, sir." A boy ran up the steps and picked up the door to lean it against the opening. He stopped and looked out into the streets. "They're all over the city. Guards are everywhere."

William went up the steps before the other children could follow. He looked out to see the city crawling with Guards. Each was going after the children first, taking little care with how they handled their work. "Children, class is dismissed today. Go home. I'm sure your parents are worried. And whatever you do, do not aggravate the guards. Be respectful, for your own sake." He was worried about his own son, and his son was twenty-three.

CHAPTER 14: LEARNING FROM DONNA

WHEN the dawn came, everyone at Donna's woke to breakfast already made. On the table, in the same room as the sleeping trio, was a pile of freshly cooked meats and breads and some fruit. It was perfect, for the sausage that was provided was as hot as anything Markus had ever tasted, which meant the others were happy eaters. The only thing missing from the table was the hostess. Donna was nowhere to be found that morning. She had set up breakfast and left them to get around on their own. Of course, they knew she had a shop to keep, but Treb knew she was probably still embarrassed to be seen by any of them right now.

Once they finished eating, Crystal and Markus sat by the fire, and she showed him some of her best spells for healing.

"Would you stop grinning like that? You aren't paying attention," Crystal said, quietly breaking Markus' goofy stare.

"I was just thinking about what we did last night."

Crystal could not contain the grin on her face. "I don't know what came over me. I just couldn't help myself. I'm sorry if I—"

Markus stopped her by placing his hand on hers. "You have nothing to be sorry about. I liked it. Perhaps a little warning next time, but . . ."

She looked down, and her tail wagged a little against the floor. "So, you want a next time?"

"Of course. I . . . well . . . I do like you." He tried not to sound like a child, but he *was* only sixteen.

Crystal looked him in the eyes. "I . . . like you, too."

"What are you two doing over here?" Treb asked as he came over to check on the fire.

Markus let go of her hand as quickly as he could and even scooted back a few more inches. "Uh, nothing. Just learning some healing magic, that's all." He sounded as guilty as he felt.

Crystal nodded as she hastily picked up her book to look at the next spell. "Yeah, that's it. I'm teaching him about this spell. Asja."

Treb looked at Markus, not as menacingly as he might have five days ago when he first brought him into the village, but still with distrust. "Shouldn't you be trying to interpret that Codex?"

"I don't have any idea how to even start. I've looked at it over and over, and nothing even begins to make sense."

Treb shook his head. "That map simply leads us into the Barren Mountains, a place dangerous to be at even the best of times. We really do need to know where to go from there. Maybe you could ask Donna to help you figure it out."

"Donna?" Markus hadn't thought of her.

"She's a wizard too, and one who went to college. She might know something of the ancient language."

"That makes sense, but I'm not sure if I should be telling everyone about our mission."

Crystal closed her book on one finger to keep her place. "I don't believe telling her would be dangerous. She's been evading the Royal Guard for four years. I doubt she'll be turning us in or spreading around rumors."

"It's worth a try."

Treb looked at his little girl seated on the floor, as she pretended to read the same page over and over, probably waiting for her overprotective father to leave. "Honey, why don't you and I go see if we can get some of the supplies we need?"

"I need to teach Markus more stuff. Can't you and Mother go out and get the supplies?"

Treb had an ingrained urge to get her away from interested boys, and he couldn't deny it. "I just think you two need some time apart. You spend too much time together."

Markus was about to protest, when Kiin interceded. "Treb, dear, let them work on their magic stuff. We can go get the supplies."

Treb looked at his wife and then back at his little girl. The idea of leaving her here with Markus, a boy she had already kissed, was almost too much for him. Then he recalled that moment on the hill as they hid from Morris. Markus had displayed real honor then and genuine care for Crystal. Perhaps a little trust had been earned. "All right. You two stay inside and keep away from the Guards."

Markus was shocked. He had expected more arguments. "Okay, sure."

Kiin took her husband's hand and walked him out of the room.

Treb stood with his wife in the next room. She stopped him and gave him a good kiss. He did not fight it, and once it was over he had to ask, "What was that for?"

She ran her hands down his back and gave his rear a playful squeeze, something she always did after a good kiss. "I'm so proud of you. You didn't fight back. Are you beginning to see that Markus isn't going to hurt her?"

Treb looked back at the doorway, though he could not see into the room. "Yeah. I think I can trust him. He honestly likes her and wants to keep her safe."

Kiin walked away and picked up the bowl that was still on the floor from where Treb had knocked it off when Donna had become a bit too frisky. "After what happened last night, I was worried about you."

227

Treb looked at her as she was examining the bowl, which only brought back to his mind the incident last night. "Oh, you know what happened?"

She laughed at him, still thinking of when they had both watched the kids kiss. "Of course; we were both there."

"Uh . . . are you angry?"

Kiin set the bowl down and turned to him with a thoroughly confused look. "Of course not. I think it was sweet. Perhaps a little awkward, but still sweet."

"You . . . thought . . . it was sweet?" He was confounded. "You don't think she was pushing a little too hard?"

Kiin shrugged. "No. Actually, I thought I might give her a few pointers about next time."

"Next time!" He was aghast.

"Shush!" She put her finger on his mouth. "Don't worry the kids. Yes, next time. I think if she's going to attempt a relationship with someone that's not of her race, she needs to know a few things."

Treb was disgusted, shocked, and more than confused. "I would think you would discourage it. Didn't it shock you?"

"I already told you I was fine with it. In fact, it might happen again tonight, and if it does, she needs to know how far to go and not to go."

Treb sat down on his bed. "Kiin, dear, you're scaring me."

"Okay, I don't think we're on the same page. What are you talking about?"

Treb frowned at her and decided it would be best to make her explain first. "What are *you* talking about?"

Kiin gestured back to the den. "The kids. Crystal needs to know a few things about kissing and what is unacceptable and what is acceptable. She also needs to know the differences between the Humankind and Rakki when it comes to romance and stuff like that. What were you talking about?"

Treb looked around and gulped. He had half a moment to come up with a good explanation that made sense. "Well . . . I . . . was just confused. That is all. You talking to her about that romantic stuff is fine. It's girl stuff."

Kiin knew her man better than that. He was hiding something, and sooner or later, she would find out. But it was not the time to push, so she let it go. "At least you and Markus already talked about girls. He knows what to expect from Rakki girls, fangs and all."

Treb frowned at her. "You listened in, didn't you?"

She laughed and patted his shoulder armor. "Honey, I'll always know what I need to know when it comes to this family. Don't worry; you didn't get yourself in too much trouble."

"I'm in trouble?" His deep, manly voice suddenly changed into the meager squeak of a husband in trouble.

"Yes, but we will talk about it later. Now we need to get our supplies. I don't want to spend too much time here—too many guards around to find Crystal and Markus."

Treb rose and followed her with absolute obedience. They passed Donna when they got up the stairs. She was heading down and looked particularly terrified when she passed Treb and Kiin. The flush of red in her cheeks seemed to have made itself a permanent home. Treb felt bad for her, but Kiin was left to wonder what was going on between them.

Donna walked into the room where she had insulted Treb. She felt like a complete fool. She wanted a man, but her attempts at flirting were always awkward and clumsy. However, she hadn't accidentally gone after a married man before. What had she been thinking?

"Donna? Are you in there?" Markus called out.

She fixed her face so she wasn't frowning anymore and put on a smile. Coming around the corner, she found the kids working hard, learning magic. "Can I help you?"

Markus looked at the Codex and thought for a moment about

telling her about it. "Well, I was wondering if you could help with some magical stuff. Neither of us have done any work with real wizards before."

Crystal corrected him. "I grew up with wizards, but they didn't really teach me anything other than medical magic."

Donna was glad to help them. It might help earn some forgiveness from Treb for her actions. Besides, it was nice to be with other wizards again. "Sure. What can I do?" She came over and sat down on the floor, crossing her legs. She noticed the book Crystal had. "Oh, you have some healing spells. I can certainly help with that, especially medicinal potion blending."

Crystal held out her little notebook. "It's not much. Just some stuff I learned in our library. I use it to practice my magic."

"May I?" Donna took the book from her and looked at the spells and notes Crystal had written down. "Goodness, you have a strong grasp on this already. Who taught you about healing magic?"

Crystal brushed her hair out of her face and looked away in humility. "Well, I learned most of it from books and personal practice. My parents were healers before they were taken from me. My father was a good surgeon wizard, and my mother was the best healing wizard anyone had ever known."

Donna flipped through the book. The notes beside each spell

were very well thought out. "This looks like the work of a final year student in the healing school of the college. Where did you practice? I know not all of these notes are just transcribed from books. Some are your own thoughts and opinions about healing magic."

"I was allowed to practice in the infirmary of my village. I wasn't given any of the serious cases, so I couldn't make horrible mistakes. The doctors and nurses of the infirmary were good friends of my parents and offered to help me when I came into my powers."

Donna handed back the book. "You'll make a fine doctor one day. All I could teach you would be about potion mixing for healing arts."

"Oh, I'd like to learn about that. The books gave recipes and some notes, but all stated I needed to practice with a potion master."

"Yes, mixing potions can be tricky without a teacher there. A little too much of an ingredient and, *boom*, there goes the house." Donna grimaced at the memories of some of the things she had accidentally blown up in her practicing years. "I can show you a few things. But we must be careful. Anything that uses magic must be hidden so they don't know of it."

"I understand. Maybe before we leave, I can learn a few things."

Markus took the Codex from his side. "I have questions that aren't about healing or potions."

Donna's jaw dropped and her eyes were fixed on the book. "Where did you get that?"

"The Rakki have protected it for a long time. The wizard who wrote it told them it was for a special occasion. We're hoping it'll lead to answers about the Dragonwand." He waited for her, knowing that simply saying Dragonwand would bring out something. He was not sure what, exactly, though.

Donna was quiet for a moment and then looked at him. "What do you know of the Dragonwand?"

Crystal started, "We are—"

But Markus stopped her. He gave Donna a deadly serious gaze. "What would you do if you found it?" was the only question he could think of that would help him know how to answer her question.

She looked away and thought about it for a moment. "I cannot say. I know the King has ordered it to be found. I also know that we haven't been told the truth about it by the palace; someone wants it for evil purposes."

Markus then asked, "Do you know where it is?"

Donna nodded. "Yes, but only by legend. It's said to be in the Dragon Citadel. Unfortunately, no one knows where to find that place."

Markus opened the book. "This book is supposed to lead us to the Citadel. But we don't know how to interpret it. Can you?" He set it in front of her.

Donna was in awe of the Codex. To see such an artifact in person was breathtaking. "It's in such good condition. It must be protected by magic. Wow, this is the ancient tongue."

Crystal asked again, "Can you read it?"

Donna picked up the book, and an envelope fell out, which Markus quickly grabbed and put away. Donna asked, "What was that?"

"Just notes; nothing important." He sounded a little defensive.

Donna went on, "No, I'm afraid the only ones who can read this language are the Ancients. This text has to be deciphered through some magical method, but I don't know what it is. Each book and scroll was enchanted with a different encryption key."

Markus let out a defeated sigh. "Why would Tolen send me on a quest without giving me anything more than this stupid wand? I don't know how to do this. We're going to get lost in the mountains, while the King does who knows what to Gallenor."

Donna broke through his angry mutterings. "He gave you this, too." She pointed to the book.

Markus corrected her, "No, the Rakki had that hidden and gave it to me to help. Tolen only gave me a wand."

Donna amended, "See this?" She pointed to a bit of scribbled writing in the front of the Codex. "I may not have the deciphering spell for the rest of this, but this isn't an encrypted word; it's his name in the ancient tongue."

Markus frowned. "How do you know that?"

"Tolen the Wise was the Chief Wizard over the college when I was an instructor there. Though none of us knew he was an Ancient, he *did* write this as his name when he signed important documents. We all believed he was just showing off."

"Did you know him well?" Crystal asked.

"Not as well as I would've liked. He left the school right after the King's head wizard, Hallond, came to the college and informed us that dark forces were at work in Gallenor again. I had only been an instructor for a year at that point."

"What dark forces? Did he say?" Markus wanted to know more about what they were up against.

"Dark magic has always been in Gallenor since the War. Imps are made of it, and so are a few other undesirable creatures. In the past ten years, the amount of dark magic creatures roaming the lands has increased, and this certainly got a lot of people's attention. Then Hallond said the dragon statue outside of Thendor Castle was gaining power and slowly reanimating."

Markus looked away, confused. "The statue?"

"Yes. For generations, the Head Council of magic had informed all of Gallenor that the dragons were the responsible party in the War, and that the statue was the last dragon. He was stopped just before our destruction. I believed that, until the day I escaped." Donna hugged her arms around herself as she recalled that terrible day.

Crystal softly asked, "What happened?"

"The first order to secure all wizards was only for the college and Thendor province. That was about a year and a half before the rest of Gallenor was commanded to surrender their wizards to the Guard. All wizards were to be put in the Pale Labyrinth for the safety of Gallenor. I knew this was wrong. The Royal Guard descended on the college in force, to enforce the new law. Some of the wizards followed willingly, and some fought back. I ran.

"Five of us got away, and we were met by Tolen. He said he had a place in the valley that was hidden from the eyes of the King. But as we traveled, four of the others were captured. Tolen managed to keep me safe and told me the dragon statue and the Dragonwand were not evil as was believed for generations. He also said that those two items were the means to end the threat of dark forces in Gallenor, and that he needed a wizard strong enough to finish his mission."

"Why didn't he do it himself?" Markus asked. "Or ask you to do it?"

Donna seemed a little ashamed of herself. "Tolen was old—older than any of us ever believed possible. He knew he couldn't complete this mission of his. For years, he had been searching for the right wizard for the job. He must have known these dark times would come long before any of us were aware, for he had been searching since before the decree."

"My grandmother," Markus muttered.

"Huh?"

Markus explained, "Tolen told me he sent out the call to my grandmother and then my father to follow their hearts and finish his mission. But they refused their magical heritage and did not listen. He must have thought my family could do this."

"Yes." Donna had an epiphany. "For some reason, your family must have it within them to finish this mission. I offered my service to him, but he told me I wasn't the right person. I can't say it didn't hurt me to hear that, but I also knew if I failed, all could be lost. Tolen told me to go—that the King was only interested in finding him. This was before the widespread decree was ordered. He said Stillwater would be a safe place, and I could prove useful here. I came here and built a potion business and waited for the day Tolen would call upon me to help him, or that I . . ." She then realized her encounter with Markus and his companions may have not been chance. After a pause, she continued. "I would find what I needed to find. That my part in all of this would come about." She was looking at Markus with an astonished expression.

Markus was also surprised. "So, he had this planned all along, that clever fool."

"He was no fool. Tolen was the wisest person in all of Gallenor." Donna would always defend Tolen.

"If Tolen was so wise," Crystal said, "why didn't he do something about this long before now? He must've been very powerful."

"I don't know. I've asked myself that a thousand times over the past four years. The only conclusion I can draw is that there's a specific timing to all of this. I just hope we aren't too late," Donna said.

Markus took the book up in his hands. "No, I won't believe that. We still have a chance to do something. I'll find the Citadel, the Dragonwand, and finish what he started. While we're still free, we have the opportunity to put an end to this."

Donna looked directly at Markus. "Let me tell you one last thing

Tolen told me. The King's mad, as is his head wizard. His goals and plans aren't for anyone's good but his own. Don't trust him or any of his loyalists, and know he'll do anything to stop you from completing this mission."

"We know of the King's madness," said Crystal. "One of my own kind overheard him discussing plans to destroy all the wizards held in the Labyrinth and use them to cast some sort of ancient, wicked spell."

Donna slowly put her hand over her mouth as the news sank in. She had only known that the King was mad, but she had no idea how bad it was. "Oh, no. All my friends, my family."

Crystal nodded. Then she turned her face away as she tried not to become terribly depressed, thinking of her parents being killed like that. "My family, too."

Markus took Crystal's hand. "I won't let them do that. For you, I'll believe we still stand a chance. Otherwise, we'll all be lost in regret and fear."

Donna smiled at Markus. "You know something, kid? You're pretty wise."

"Thanks. I've heard that most of my life. The farmers I lived around always said I spoke with the voice of someone much older than I. Maybe that's why Tolen liked me; I sound like a wise old

man some times." He opened the book and looked at the signature.
"You know, I know that Tolen planned all of this—at least, our part
in this journey. The wand, this book, meeting you . . . the
coincidence is too great. I think the only part he forgot was teaching
me how to read this stupid book."

Donna stood up, her knees creaking a little. "Don't be too sure
about that. Tolen was very wise, but sometimes those wise old fools
also liked riddles. I suspect he gave you what you need; you just
need to figure it out."

CHAPTER 15: TIME TO GO!

TREB and Kiin walked through the marketplace and found part of what they needed. Treb purchased another sleeping mat, another traveling bag, and some dried foods. Kiin got a map from someone she hoped was a reliable source. She wanted to have something handy when they went into the mountains. The back of the Codex had a general map of Gallenor, which mostly showed basic features, but not an in-depth map of specific locations.

"Are you sure you can read that?" Treb asked his wife while carrying his purchases.

Kiin opened the map a little more and turned it over a few times. She looked at a strange script of mostly long lines and some dots. "Sure, I . . . think I can. I haven't looked at Shlan script in a long time, but I know the basics."

"Great. Now we have two maps we can't read," Treb grumbled

Kiin snarled at him and showed him the map, holding it up so he had to stop walking or he would not see where he was going. "Look, at least we can determine the paths and ledges from this. The language is just added material for the traveler. I bet it's nothing more than tips on camping and a general almanac to the temperatures of the mountains during the year."

"You bet?"

She closed the map in such a way that her hand nearly hit his nose. "Fine, we can just go on blindly." Kiin walked on ahead of him.

"Honey, don't get mad." Treb ran along behind her with all his loot still cluttering up his arms.

Kiin stopped and turned around. "Don't worry. This map will be fine. And if it is that important to you, I have an idea . . . HEY!" She waved down a Shlan woman that was walking by.

The woman gave both Rakki a confused look and stopped walking. She didn't get any closer, but gave a slight smile to acknowledge them.

Kiin ran over to her. "Hi, I'm sorry to bother you, but I need someone who can read this." She opened the map.

The woman gave Kiin a funny look and then looked down at the map. "It'sss a map of the mountainsss."

"Oh, I know that. But, I don't know what this says exactly. My Shlan is a little rusty." Kiin tried to be as pleasant as possible, because the Shlan weren't overly fond of Rakki, generally speaking.

The woman looked at the words and then thought for a second. "In common tongue, it ssssayss: Warning, impssss presssent. Higher you go, more impsss are sssseeen." It wasn't easy translating directly from Shlan basic to Gallenorian.

Treb looked at the map, and he sort of frowned at his wife. "Imps? Really?"

The woman nodded. "Yesss. I wouldn't go there. Have good day." She hurried on her way.

Treb looked at his wife with an *I told you so* look. "Temperature almanac."

"Fine. At least we have a warning. Now that I know what this says, I think I can remember more of these words." She looked deep at the maps other small notes here and there. "That says something about water, and that . . ."

Treb bumped into her on purpose to get her attention. "Kiin, look!"

Kiin looked up to see Captain Morris and three of the city Guards inspecting people at the end of the block. "Oh, no. I know exactly what that means."

Treb nodded and started to back away. "He's bound to recognize us."

"Hurry, let's get back to the shop. Hopefully he's too busy inspecting people to notice us right now." Kiin turned and followed Treb back the other way toward the potion shop.

Markus sat at the dinner table with the Codex open. After Donna left the room to check on the girl she hired to run her booth every other day, he decided he might try to figure out what would be the key to decipher the text.

Crystal read a manual containing instructions on creating magical potions Donna had lying around. It was a basic text used by the students of the college when she had taught. Crystal knew one like it was in the Rakki library, but she hadn't gotten to potion making yet in her personal studies. Lowering the book, she looked up to see Markus writing something on a piece of paper. Maybe he had an idea about deciphering.

"Hey, Markus, I do know a little about magical ciphers—something I read in the library of my village. Maybe I could help." She set the potion book down.

"No, I . . . don't need your help."

This drew her attention all the more. What was he hiding from her? She felt it was not something terribly secret, or he might not be doing it out in the open like this. So Crystal got up and quietly strolled over to him to take a look over his shoulder. When she did, she found something she had not expected. He wasn't working on the Codex; in fact, the book was closed. He was writing a letter.

Dear Mom and Dad

It has been a month and a week since I left home. I am in Stillwater, a town in the foothills of the Barren Mountains. I haven't told you yet what I am doing. I don't think I am ready to. I wanted to tell you I do love you and miss you. I . . .

Markus suddenly realized someone was reading over his shoulder. He quickly stopped and hid the letter. "Crystal! This is private."

She stepped back, but did not leave. "It's okay to miss your parents. Of all people, I know how it hurts."

Markus slowly moved the letter back out. "I . . . I realized a while back I hadn't really given thought to how they might feel. I was prepared to come home on a break or something and just tell them how great I was doing and they would be proud. At least, I would've if I'd gone to school and all this hadn't happened. When I thought about how much you would love to be able to speak to your parents again, I discovered there was still a little kid in my heart who missed his mom and dad. So I started writing them letters."

"How many have you written?" Crystal pulled over a chair and sat down beside him.

He took out the folded envelope from the Codex and lifted it to show her the stack of letters. "I started them back in your village. I didn't know how to mail them and got swept up in leaving and going on this journey. I expected to find a way to mail them in one of the villages when we would stop. I hadn't expected to be running from the authorities."

Crystal stated the obvious, but with great care. "You know, if you send those, and any of the Royal Guard catches on, they'll track them to your parents. I hate to think of what they would do."

"I thought of that and considered I would stop writing them. But I don't want to stop. It gives me the hope of seeing them again. Even if I have to hand these letters to them myself, I will."

Crystal smiled at him and rubbed his ear, something Rakki did to one another as a sign of affection. For Markus, it was just an odd sensation. "You really do have a loving heart. Even though you and your parents were angry with each other over the past few years, I know they love you. And I'm sure they know you love them as well."

He rolled his shoulders because she was sort of tickling him. "That feels weird," he said.

She quickly took her hand off of his head. "Oh, humans don't rub ears?"

"Not that I'm aware of. We whisper sweet nothings in them." He was trying to flirt, but his reference made little sense to her. So, he got sweet. He reached into the envelope and slid out a sheet of blank paper, one of the few he had left. "Why don't you write your parents something? So when you see them, you can give it to them as well."

She looked at the paper with a little curiosity. "What would I tell them?"

"Tell them what you have been doing these past four years, how much you like Treb and Kiin, and how good they have been to you. Tell them you love them and miss them. I know you will tell them all this when you see them, but writing it out sort of relaxes your heart and helps you prepare yourself for that wonderful moment."

She slid the paper back over to him. "No, not now. But I'll give it some thought. Perhaps when I'm ready, you can help me. I'm no good at writing anything that isn't technical stuff."

Markus took the paper and placed it back into the envelope. "Sure, any time you want."

Just then, Donna came in, carrying a book in her hand. "Hey, I have something for you guys." She sat down at the table with them and set the book in front of Markus.

He looked at it and realized it was a wizard's personal spell book, not unlike the little book that Crystal kept all her important spells in. "What's this?"

Donna opened it and revealed all the spells she had written into it. "This is my working spell book from when I went to the college.

You can learn a lot from the notes and the spells. It isn't a replacement for a good spell library and instructors, but it might prove useful on your journey."

Markus was thrilled and humbled. "I can't take this. A wizard's personal spell book is special to them."

She insisted by pushing it closer to him. "I want you to have it. It hasn't done me much good over the past few years, and I bet you could use a few lessons in magic. You said you didn't feel very prepared for this. This book is the collected lessons I kept when I was a student. Maybe you can be the student as well when you look at them."

Markus was very eager to take it, so his humility took a back seat. He pulled the book closer, ready to pore through it. "I'll try to do your gift justice."

"Just do your best. That's what I told every one of my students. When you learn, do your best, for anything less is cheating only you."

Markus was already reading the first page. Crystal read over his shoulder, and Donna realized she was not the center of attention any more. But just as she stood up to leave, Treb and Kiin rushed through the door.

"He's coming!" Kiin said.

Crystal gasped, but mostly at the surprise of her parents bursting through the door. "Who's coming?" she asked.

Kiin quickly came in and began to gather their stuff. "Morris."

Treb added, "There are guards everywhere, and Morris is leading them."

Markus was stacking up his books "Did he see you?"

"No," Kiin answered. "But, they're scouring the city. It won't be long before they get here."

Crystal looked at Donna. "This basement is hidden, right? We just have to stay down here. He won't find us."

Donna shook her head with a sympathetic frown. "Honey, I can't promise you'll be safe down here if they come looking."

"We can't stay," Treb reiterated. "If they discover us down here, we'll have nowhere to run. Now, get your stuff together, we have to move." He held up a bag for Crystal to help pack.

"I have an idea," Donna said, then ran up the stairs to her potion shop.

Markus tucked the Codex deep into his bag so it would be even harder to see. He asked, "What happens if they come across us out there? We can't fight all the city guards."

As Kiin tied her bag closed, she answered, "Let us worry about that."

Just then, Donna ran back into the basement den with a vial of potion. She headed straight for Crystal and Markus. "Here, take this," she urged them.

Markus looked at the nearly clear liquid. "What is it?"

She took the cork out and poured a little into her hand and carefully dabbed it on Crystal. "It's my potion that disguises you from the sensing stones. I only hope it works."

Crystal rubbed her hand on her fur where it was the wettest and spread it around a little. "You *hope* it works?"

Donna looked very afraid for them as she started working on Markus. "I formulated this for me, and I'm not all that powerful. I don't know if your magical abilities are too strong for this batch. But . . . it's the best I can do."

Treb handed Markus a bag to carry on his back, then looked at Donna. "Thank you for all you've done for us."

Donna still had a hard time looking him in the eye, though she didn't have a hard time looking at his chest. "Oh, we're not going our separate ways just yet. I'm going to lead you out of the city."

Kiin shook her head as she slid her arms into the straps of her pack. "We cannot put you in any danger."

Donna laughed at them and then started applying the potion to herself. "Listen, Tolen gave me a mission—a mission to help you. My responsibility to the wizards of Gallenor does not stop here. I will see to it that you're safe as far as I can."

Markus asked, "Does this mean you're going with us to the Citadel?"

"Yes. I have to help."

Treb shook his head. "No, that is simply not acceptable."

Donna drew a little closer to him and softly said, "I know we had a little mix-up, but I can help. This is important."

Treb whispered right back, "It has nothing to do with last night." His voice lifted so that everyone could hear him then. "It is simply not possible to have you following along. This journey is bound to be filled with dangers."

Donna laughed and patted his chest. "Honey, I can handle myself. I am, after all, a master wizard."

Kiin came over then. "Treb, she has a point. Besides, I think she could help the kids learn about magic along the way. I'm sure a teacher wouldn't be unwise."

Treb rolled his eyes, but agreed. "Fine. Just make sure to keep yourself safe."

"I am the only instructor of the college who is not dead or in that damned Labyrinth. I think I can handle myself. Now, let's get out of here as quickly as possible."

The potion master opened the secret door and led them up the stairwell to the main room of her shop. Treb was right behind her with Kiin on his tail.

Markus looked over to Crystal and saw fear bubbling in her eyes. She was still afraid of Morris and wasn't sure what to do from there. So, he softly took her hand and smiled at her. The fear seemed to simmer down when she returned his smile and followed him, her hand firmly kept by his.

Donna took a few potions from her shelves and packed them into Treb's and Kiin's bags. "When we get out of here, the best route is to go the same way you came in," she explained. "That door is hardly used and barely watched. Once we get outside of the city wall, we run like hell."

Treb watched the door carefully for any sign of the Guards coming in. "What if they have stationed Guards outside the city walls?"

Donna grinned and handed him a potion bottle. "This is a unique potion called bottled fear. Throw it at the Guards, and it will explode into a great cloud. Once they inhale it, you will look like a giant monster attacking. If they have any self-preservation in their blood, they'll flee like flies from a swatter."

Kiin took one of the bottles and gave Donna a less than enthusiastic glance. "Won't it do the same to us?"

Donna nodded. "Yup, but you know it's just an illusion; they don't. I know it'll be hard, but you're warriors. Show courage, and the fear potion won't be much of an obstacle."

Treb tucked the potion away where he could get to it quickly. "I just hope we won't need to use it. Let's move."

No sooner had they taken a step to leave, when a girl come running in. "Donna, you can't go!"

Donna held a hand up to calm her down. "Tasha, Tasha, settle down. Don't attract attention. I know you weren't quite ready for this, but the shop is yours, and I'm leaving."

Tasha shook her head. "No, it's not that. The Guards just told me the city has been locked down. No one can enter or leave. You really can't go."

"Oh, I see what you mean. Well . . . I . . . Treb?" She was at a loss for a plan.

Treb looked around. "We can't stay here. It'll be only a matter of time before they find us."

Tasha's eyes widened, as she had not actually seen the people her friend had been hiding. It was only then she realized something. "Oh my."

Donna cocked her head. "What is it?"

"That Captain Morris. He put out a sign this morning saying the King has issued a priority objective target on a boy traveling with a Rakki family. A human boy . . ." She looked at Markus. "It's you they're after."

Markus asked, "What's a priority objective?"

Kiin answered, "It means you are now the most wanted person in all of Gallenor. Every person in all the lands under the King are required to be on the lookout for you."

"Oh." Markus was stunned for a moment.

Treb looked back at Markus, then at Tasha. "What did you tell them?"

She shook her head furiously. "I didn't tell them anything. Donna told me to keep her guests a secret. I didn't even know you were the ones they were looking for."

Kiin let out a harsh sigh with a touch of a growl in it. "That Morris must be after us for evading him."

Markus began to realize his life was in real danger. "Uh, what will you do?"

Treb looked to Donna. "Are there any other secret ways out of this city? A drainage system or a crack in the wall?"

"Yes, I think there is. A group of young boys I know use an opening in the city wall on the far side to get out and play in a field. The City Guard never sealed it and don't watch over it. It will be difficult to get through, but I think we can squeeze."

Treb understood this was their only option, and he would rather die before handing his daughter over to the Guard. "Fine, lead us there." He took his Crystal's arm and held her close to him. "Stay with me while we go through the city."

Donna sort of pushed Tasha back out to the stand. "Dear, the shop's all yours. I don't know if I will ever come back. Thank you for being such a good assistant."

"Thanks. I will do you proud." Tasha hadn't been expecting this so soon, but she felt ready.

Donna smiled at her. "One last request: if they come asking about me, tell them I'm ill. When enough time has passed, tell everyone I passed away."

"No one will believe me."

Donna grinned. "I know, but the Guards will. And that's what matters. Now, don't watch me leave; I can't let them see us." With that, she hurried out with the others. All five ran down the street and out of view.

255

Tasha had seen this many of the Guard in Stillwater only one other time: the week they had carried off all the wizards they could find. Men and women had been dragged out of their homes. Several had fought and were killed in the street, and the sight of their blood still haunted her nightmares. Her heart sank as she pictured Donna lying dead in the street, just like that man who had been stuck by five arrows in front of their shop. "Please make it out alive," she whispered.

ABOUT THE AUTHOR

Daniel Peyton was born in Stillwater, Oklahoma, and now resides near the Smokey Mountains in East Tennessee. He is an honorary member of the Sigma Alpha Iota, professional performer with the Miygai Ryu Nosho Kai, and a longtime member of the Embroiderers Guild of America. Daniel is an award winning stitcher, graphic artist, stage performer, and cook. The verities of experiences have helped him develop rich worlds and characters for his fiction works. Since the fourth grade he has never stopped penning stories for the entertainment of others.

MORE BOOKS FROM DANIEL PEYTON

LEGACY OF DRAGONWAND BOOK II

www.cosbymediaproductions.com

Printed in Great Britain
by Amazon

84957656R00154